DONALD

McSWEENEY'S
SAN FRANCISCO

www.mcsweeneys.net

Copyright © 2011 Eric Martin and Stephen Elliott

Cover illustration by Simon Rippingale

McSweeney's and colophon are registered trademarks of McSweeney's,
a privately held company with wildly fluctuating resources.

ISBN: 978-1-936365-25-8

DONALD

Eric Martin & Stephen Elliott

1

He is reading. The library is empty except for two limp scholars by the window. Look at their posture. How much butt would he have kicked here? The place is old, the oldest library in an old town. It's too dark but the scholars don't seem to mind. They're twenty years younger than him, but he could outwrestle them. Them and every scholar in his weight class in every library in the world. His scholarly skills are not shabby, either. He reads like lightning. His hands are always moving, wringing ideas from the page. "Like a perv," an assistant aide's assistant once observed, and if by that she meant the body is the mind then fine, nice jab, he could give a rat's how it looked. There's a reason she was an assistant's assistant. A reason generals and bureaucrats waited for a turn with him, turns that by well-publicized accounts were not all pleasant. But was he fair? He was so fair. He was so fair he screwed himself all the time.

He does not know the kid who sits down across from him, leaning two pointy elbows on the table. Six feet tall, soft 170, swallow's nest of hair. The girl watches from three steps behind. He can't tell if she's ridiculously beautiful or if that's just what girls always look like when they're twenty-five. Good lord god almighty.

"Sir," the kid says. "Good afternoon."

Silence circles the drain. The kid's got something. Head still. Hands away from his face. "Quick," he tells them, finally, "I'm old, you know. Ha ha ha." He smiles at the girl. Her short blond hair is blinding atop her cream-colored cashmere sweater. She smiles back. Her mouth looks very organized and fertile, and she looks like she knows her boy's set to get reamed, and that's fine with her.

"Not that old," the kid says. "I've followed your career with interest." Here comes the nervous hand now across lips and chin, unable to hold its position. No ring, no watch, thin fingers.

"Well hasn't it been interesting."

"Start to finish," says the kid.

"Oh am I finished?" His best grin, tops and bottoms. He winks at the girl and she doesn't look away. "Absolutely right," he says. "I've sure been blessed in that department but it's all over now, like the good song says." From the shelves, thousands of books lean down on them, oozing leather, arcana, decay. "I won't waste your time," the kid says. His voice is nasal and he tries to go down low to hide it. Your voice is your voice, there's nothing to be done. "The commission is going to request that you testify. We would like to flesh some things out prior, as your schedule permits."

"What's this *we*, white man?" He checks to see if she gets the reference, or anything for that matter. She's grown stony. Her sweater is beginning to look scratchy.

"I'm ghosting the report," the kid says. "There are omissions in your account. We're looking to set baselines for productive dialogue."

The library is listening now. Wide knotty floorboards stand on tiptoe, and gated presses lean around them. A shelver watches, gripping two black centuries in his hands. The scholar studying trench songs clicks his pencil. Time eases off like a dusk wind. He's missed this.

He idly slides a book about Interwar naval innovation across the table. "I'm retired," he says. The kid is trying to maintain eye contact like he learned it just last week. Get a name. Don't look away until you've logged the color of their eyes. The girl's are grey, the kid's turd brown. He doesn't care about their names. "How retired I am is reading books less pertinent than the crap you took this morning. Pardon my."

The girl winces. She looks like she remembers that crap well. There's something familiar about her. Who? Someone's daughter. Her thin top lip is half-pointy, like his successor's come to think of it, or maybe not, it could be nothing, except it can't be nothing the way scorpions are scrabbling through his throat. This library is supposed to be members only, military and safe. Who let them in here?

"There are things in this report," the kid says, "things that are going to break hell loose, and I do want—the commission, we—to give you due chance for answers and the record."

His successor's daughter watches to see how the old man takes it. His thinning hair is parted. His undershirt is dry. He glances at her and she smiles again—nope, the mouth is different, too big and garish, too unserious—and he smiles back. A glut of smiles as if they're sipping cocktails instead of starting the gorilla dance. Perhaps she's never attended a reaming. There are two real kinds of people in this world. Deep down, she must know that her boy is neither of them.

"The record." He pushes on his rimless glasses, tilts his head, and gives the kid his strangler look. "Aren't these books the record, all around us?" The kid was not brought up to see books as wholes, only collections of data that could be boiled down, context stripped out. He could know the kid's age, the kid's cholesterol, the kid's genome and test scores, the diameter of the kid's unit, and yet would he know the kid? "You want to add to the record? What's the question? Ask me. Now." He uncurls a pinky and wiggles it. The girl looks like his own wife.

"Okay," answers the boy, and he knows he's made a big mistake.

The girl doesn't look like his wife. The girl is slender and blue-eyed but she doesn't look fun. It's the face shape that's the same. A circle composed of perfect little squares, round and rectangular at once. He's met movie stars possessed of such-shaped faces. He has met dictators' wives. But not many. His wife has aged comprehensively, but he still sees that shape, even when he's far away, even with his arms, legs, and eyes closed tight around her, even if conditions on the ground have changed.

"The practices you authorized," the kid begins, "have always been the exception to the rule, the ugly facet of what nations do to survive and thrive." The kid is angry, and his anger has smoothed his jitters away. Even his nasal voice sounds cleared up by adrenaline. "But you made it the rule. You called it legitimate. You sat next to the throne and offered pre-forgiveness for grave sin. And the world will never forgive us that."

The kid's blood is about to slough the skin off. If he wasn't such a kid this is when he'd call security, but this kid? This? These are his enemies now? This guy instead of the suicidal hostile or the one-legged mountainman on horseback cum machine gun? The hubris. And yet he had done it, too. Sitting in a library writing treatises on factory seizures and executive power.

He leans back twisty in his chair, belly out, shoulders wide, chin up, offering his nape. "You two married?" Triangles of light and shadow are moving across the broad oak table, poking their long fingers into the old biographies. It's going on four. He's got a drive ahead of him, dinner plans, a wife and guests. The kid and girl are wilting. "Married. Two. You." The kid doesn't move and the girl rolls in her bottom lip. "Not my business. Absolutely right." The kid is someone's son, but who isn't? "My life, on the other hand, has been a public life, and so my life is now your business. Your report. The book you're no doubt writing, as I am. Your history in progress." He breathes in deeply through his nose, takes in the musk of old books and fear. "Characterized by excellent verbs and a personal touch. A wealth of secondary sources from the public domain. Your perspective as I guess a citizen. As I guess a man." The kid is someone's grandson and every boy is someone's grandson. "Who has faced the threats and opportunities of this age and other larger stuff, with resolve and a profound sense of those who came before." The girl is smiling. Her mouth is doing something at least, jagging at the sides.

"You are going to have to answer," says the kid. His young throat beats like a jogging heart. "Things have changed."

"They always do," he tells the kid, "but never as much or fast as people think." He leans forward across the table and spreads his arms in front of him, hands joined in a power triangle. "Tell me who you are."

"I've written— "

"No. Something real. A decision you made." He glances at the girl. "A real one."

The kid brushes his hair out of his eyes and looks, for that time it takes a person to push hair from the middle of the forehead toward the left ear, about twelve years old. Late afternoons perched on a thick branch over the garage. Kick the can with his sister in the neighborhood. Smear the queer. Stealing gum. Lighting weeds with matches. Five. Nine. Twelve. A handstand on the gunnels of a canoe, diving off the NO DIVING sign. Days of the body. "What are you talking about?" the kid says.

"That's what I thought." Down there in the kid's eyes, Donald sees broad leaves of intelligence but rooted in such soft soil that it might as well be sand. A zen garden. With a few green wisps that will blow flat at the first breath of wind. The world they live in is a blustery place. This is the son of a father who never went to war. There's a little war in the girl, maybe from her father, or maybe because every beautiful girl has glimpsed the natural state of man, at least the part that would rape her if it could. "Tell me," he says to the girl, "he had to choose between his sick mother and his career. Or he won't marry you but made you give up a job. He put a dog down. He sent a buddy off to jail. You betrayed him, he forgave you. Tell me there's something that's happened in his life but do not ask me what I mean by *real*. Because if you don't know that, you really don't know anything. Success is the exception. Failure is the rule. The record," he tells the kid, pounding the table in front of him, a seismic event that ripples through the hall, rattling the books and cages and centuries, "the record is unlikely to be kept by the likes of you."

The kid's mouth pops open like a bottom-feeding fish. His plan has not survived contact with the enemy. The enemy is never who you think it is, and you are seldom who you think you are. That's what the girl is ruminating as the light now stabs her cheek, a late, low p.m. icicle of sun that points out inexpert flakes of makeup. What a waste. "Get married," he says. "Get married, have a family, children, hit the beach, let them run naked. Write poetry about sex and rock n' roll. Paint, play tennis, find some land. What are you waiting for? What are you doing here? The world's not getting any nicer, is it?"

"You should have been a source of restraint," the kid says, his voice dipped and thick now. "And you were not a source of restraint. You should have been. You used to be. I want to know why."

"We are not what's wrong with the world," he assures the kid. But the kid has surprised him. You used to be? Like he's a cop gone bad betraying his partner in some hackneyed flick? There's a reason the kid got in here. Find out. "People are seeing things they've never seen before. So let those of us who can deal with it deal with it. The rest of you should find some happiness where you can."

The kid snorts. His nose sounds clogged again. It's crooked, but not like he broke it. Crooked like a sick tree. "I'm not here to— "

"My daughter," he cuts the kid off, "told me once that it takes everyone to make a happy day. Nine years old." She's middle-aged now, gracious, grown and long, a happy housewife who could have done anything. Her choices weren't good but she made those choices work, except the marriage, of course, but he could have told her that. Did tell her. She could have had anyone. She was like her mother. Guys stuck to her like glue. There was something childish and poetic about her. Sweet, popular, laid-back, cool, courteous, gracious, accepting, pretty, skinny. Her weaknesses a glut of trust and dearth of judgment. Right ladder, wrong wall. She'd run away to the sunny West to study history but came back home—the only one who had—and now look at her! A mother to her children and to other children, on the board of countless schools and education projects, a philanthropist, a caretaker, although was she ever as wise as she was as a child? "This wise little girl lived a pretty comfortable life, you know, and she still knew how difficult it is, the perfect storm of happiness. And the thing is, I would say that I'm an optimist, but I've always thought the other way of putting it was that it only takes one jerk to crud things up for everyone, and that means you have to avoid or isolate or neutralize that bastard best you can. If he's ready to strap a bomb to his chest and kill innocents? Women, children, civilians? Poison them, infect them, crumble your cities, make you die and suffer any way he can with whatsoever he can get his hands on? When you're nine, you're looking at the world as a circle of playmates for happy days ahead, but none of us are nine here. You go out into the world?" The clock above her head is screaming at him. "Happiness can happen, but there's always—*always*—some vicious animal out there waiting. And after him, there's another." He hasn't felt like this in a while, filling a room, leaving just the tiny last nooks for them, the slits and grottos. "There's another and another, and people like you need people like me to take care of them for you and shoulder the cost, because you? You people?" He reaches across the table so quickly that the kid can't even flinch. He holds the kid's hand, palms the long thin fingers, and presses them gently flat. Then he shakes his head on its slowest setting, softly, side to side.

His left knee pops as he stands but he makes sure it doesn't register across his igneous face. The spell holds. He can still get out of here before he turns into an old fart again. "I hope," he tells the girl, "you two get out there and prove me wrong." She is beautiful after all, not like his wife but in her own way, and he's glad she was standing there to help him be his better self. But it's undeniable: the kid is on the wrong side, the girl's got the wrong boy, and he, unless some extraordinary piece of luck strikes, is going to be late for dinner.

2

There is traffic in town. The town has grown too busy and too precious, and he's not entirely without blame. His moving here caused a minor stir. Then his buddy followed suit, with motorcades, road closures, midnight helicopters, no-fly zones, no-sail zones. Although their presence here means less now than it once did, the second-home weekender crowd keeps growing. The real estate is bust-proof.

Evening strolls in cool and green with a sea breeze flicking at late summer leaves and lolling over cars and churches that tonight look extra freshly painted. People walk. People wave. It's that kind of place. A man sells cooked crabs and flirts with your wife. A man tells dirty jokes from behind the bar about goats, priests, and God's golden axe. A bed-and-breakfast widow frets over her thriving lawn. The ice cream shack teens are white-teethed and deeply tanned, and although they no longer name new flavors after him and his buddy, they still giggle when he visits and are gracious with his wife. Even the cutesy crappy stores of cutesy crap can't ruin this place, not yet. History grounds it. Nature muscles in. If you live here, there's no reason to hit town proper very often, which is just the way he and his wife and buddy and most of their neighbors like it.

He parks in the white gravel lot next to the blue real estate bunker and crosses the street to the restaurant. It's the kind of fancy one. The food is very good. His wife will order the asparagus goat cheese beets thing with the lobster risotto, and he'll have the Caesar and the duck. Their neighbors are joining them tonight. He had forgotten. Gone are the high-voltage days of being late on official business. She's put up with plenty and it wasn't all out of love for him. Their neighbors are okay but not great. Boats and birds, he thinks. Ed's just back from his big trip. He'll have a joke about mystery meat and the bank and the bad guys' strippers. Listen. Talk less, laugh more, listen.

He spots them sitting in the corner and does his best to look contrite without the frowny face that the whole world finds hilarious. "My goodness," he says, "I'm so sorry. Peggy. Ed. Gosh. Forgive me. It sure is wonderful to see you." He sits quickly, leaning over to kiss his granite wife. She looks at him but does not look at him. He considers kissing her again. Or licking her. He considers going senile right before their eyes.

"If I had your spread?" says Ed, "No way I'd shlep up to the city!" Ed bucks his big teeth in self-immolating humor. "Five chimneys and no study?"

"Oh," says Peggy, "now don't you worry." She sends him a lefty wink-caress. "A chance to gossip a little bit."

"Well I sure am deeply sorry, truly, I do hate to be the cause of an imperfect evening."

"Some," Ed sings out in a tenor that surprises him, "some im*perrrrr*fect evening." The retired lawyer grins, jiggling the ice in his empty gin glass. "You may see a— "

"Guess you just got some making up to do," cuts in Peggy with a fake stern look.

"Guess I do," he says, sneaking another glance at his wife. The welcome scold is over. They may be retired from public life but her perfect balance of real and mannered are still on display.

"I'd have him drop and give me fifty," his wife tells the mezzanine, "except he would like that." She wrinkles her nose like a newborn. "He thinks he's still twenty-six."

"Thirty-three." He rolls back his sleeve and pumps a muscle.

"Oh please do make him do it," Peggy says. "You too, Ed, you miscreant."

"What did *you* do, Ed?"

"What happens in the hinterlands," Ed says, "stays in the hinterlands."

Now they're off and running, and the men swap stories about travelling the savage yet strategic theaters of conflict, and he tries to let Ed carry them, except he knows that one of the stories is going to be about the banquet with the horse head and foreign dignitaries rolling out the happy-ending mud massage, so he tries to steer them toward the mountain vulture and a rare horned owl he thinks will interest Peggy. It does. It certainly does. Together they fantasize about a trip out through the great steppes with birding sherpas and all the time in the world, because what a shame it is that history and ideology have been so unkind to that part of the world, a land astonishing in myriad ways, not least from an equestrian perspective, which would be the real way to see it, except you'd have to hogtie Ed and Peggy to the horse—not everyone's cowfolk you know—when suddenly their champagne and crab cakes and risotto arrive.

"Sure beats a bloody horse head," says Ed, tucking in with gusto.

"Ed." Peggy tilts her bubbly at her husband like a billy club.

He waits for Ed's big mouth to clear and then sits up extra straight. "To health and home and family. And friends." He clinks with Peggy and with Ed—who forgets to meet his eyes—and then leans in to press his forehead briefly against his wife's, breathing in her hyacinth and decay. She recoils but then lets his weight find hers, and when they clink he squints *I love you* into her because he does love her. And how does he know? He knows because he would finally rather be alone with her than have anything else back. They can have their quiet matters of life and death. It is time for him to dig with her and sit intertwined and silent. They've arrived. She is the most important thing he does every day. He leans back, still feeling her pressure against his forehead, warm with her skin, their lives, and his choice.

"Oh my," she says. Not to him this time but to the champagne. It looks like ice washed in gold, with perfect beads of bubbles skipping to the surface. But the fact is it does not matter why she's happy. She's happy. The table's beautiful. Their health is pretty good. Frogs and tides and insects serenade them every night through wide refurbished windows of a grand old house that's stood the test of time. They raised great children, who raised great children. They've served. They'll leave this world better than they found it. That's a lot. That will have to be enough. The time for wanting more must pass.

"And the memoir?" Ed wriggles his fingers obscenely.

"Having a ball," he says. He forks a corner of crab cake and dissolves it in his mouth. "Hell of a luxury, writing books."

"Hmmm," his wife says. "No one would know by the noisy anguish caused."

"Well I do enjoy the research anyway. Total control. Total responsibility. The facts and sources."

"You?" Ed winks at outer space.

"I can't wait to read it," Peggy says.

"She wants to know if she's in there."

"I'm not sure I am," his wife says.

"Time to lobby. I'm open to plain graft."

"Well." Peggy sticks her left cheek and boob at him. "It's going to be a huge hit."

"Very kind of you," he says. He likes Peggy all right, except when she disgusts him.

The dining room fills and empties and fills again. They're getting along fine. His wife has forgiven him, at least above the water line, although he wouldn't be surprised to see sharks below slipping through holes in the hull. Ed is drunk and funny, legs spread, black belt half-buckled, beige pants too tight. Peggy is Peggy. When his wife leaves for the bathroom, he feels a rodent tugging at his pant cuff, and looks down to see Peggy's black tortoiseshell French pump buzzing north. He laughs out loud, pushes back from the table, turns a protective flank and crosses his legs in plain view, catching the eye of a young couple watching from across the room. What did they see? What do they think?

The couple quickly looks away, their mouths electric with buried laughter. They are older than his grandchildren but younger than his children, the same generation as the kid and his girl from the library. His grandchildren, with their tattoos and cultural cocktails and technological assumptions, they might actually have a chance, but this generation in between is a generation of true losers. By the time he was their age, he'd married, served his country, won four elections, managed broad constituencies, and was raising three children. What are they doing? Writing books? About war? What could they possibly know? A man who has not even faced the marital responsibility of his honor and faith and duty to one person, what did he imagine the decisions were that must be made, day after day, year after year? If that kid had said to him: I decided to pursue my dreams instead of taking care of my sick mother; I decided to leave the woman I did not love even though we had a child; I decided to protect a friend although he had done something unforgivably wrong—then fine! Listening! I've sent men to their death and held the strangled eyes of their mothers. I've crossed men I admire and earned their hatred forever. I've caused strange innocents harm to protect my innocents. I've bucked age-old conventions to save lives. I've risked my family's happiness for personal ambition, time and time again. I have.

His wife has returned to the table. She pulls gently at her earlobe, runs a finger down her cheek, and he is catapulted through millennia—okay, decades—to their earliest days, the midland city, their favorite sport, their favorite team, limp summer heat, their playful signs for the unspoken and even the taboo. Come get me. Let's slip out of here. Alone. Amends. She knows what he's risked, but why on earth would he risk it still? Why not get to dinner on time? Why not sit out back and read and talk and doze off holding hands? What's wrong with him? Why can't he stop? He wants to know how she could really know him and believe that he'd stop. They are at a golden impasse. They are at dinner. They are in the demi-country at their semi-country house. That's the problem. What a wonderful dinner. What a wonderful night. Good night. Good night.

Together they watch Ed and Peggy lurch into their taupe sedan. It's a short drive. They'll be fine. He takes his wife's hand and they cross the street.

"Where's your car?" he says.

"I walked."

"You walked?" A bolt of alarm rocks him. Cancer. Insanity.

"I knew you'd be late. But that way I wouldn't know for sure until I got there. It's a lovely walk."

"Far." He pictures her frowning down the road's sloping shoulder past Tuckbox and Southwind and Banbury. He tries not to sound relieved.

"Far." She's just pissed off.

He opens her door for her. If in doubt, don't. If still in doubt, do what's right. "Let's fly out to the ranch," he says before he knows it. "Tomorrow. You know what I mean." She laughs, not kindly. "I'm different," he says. "You think I'm some bird of prey but I can also be a horse. Or a mountain goat. *Braaah.*"

She looks at him now for what feels like the first time tonight. With her head tilted up at him, the skin on her neck tightens and the light feathers her silver and white split ends. In his mind's eye he sees the hackneyed word again written in four block-letter caps. He'll say it soon if she doesn't.

"Maybe you could be," she says instead. "If we never came back."

He considers the girl from the library and what she'll look like when she's old. We all decay but she'll fare well. The kid without a chin's in trouble, that crooked kid is screwed, but the girl will keep her grace just like his wife has, and if she is as fair to the boy as his wife has been to him, the boy will be far luckier than he deserves. He has no idea what kind of life the boy can give her—as a committee lackey, as a righteous little prick—but happiness is not out of the question. Astonishing. He'll say it if she doesn't. "I love you," he tells his wife. "Let's go. I want to try."

3

It's an infamous house. The home of a notorious slave breaker, where one of history's most famous slaves was sent. It feels like more than a house. A little pool, a stable. And there's an inlet from the river that winds up to the backside, culminating in a small dock.

His wife is already in bed. He's sitting at his table, the lamp the only light on in the house, its glow pressed against the window. His wife, he thinks, pressing one thick hand on his papers. Did he waste time? he asks himself. There's no answer to that question. Time is not yours to waste. But now, in their old age, it's okay. He writes. He has the book. He has his small foundation. Soon he'll go upstairs. He'll change into his pajamas, brush his teeth, wash his face. He'll crawl next to her, cup his knees behind her knees. They didn't used to sleep like this. Or first they did, in the early years, and then they didn't. But recently, since his retirement, they've started sleeping this way again. Her hair in his nose doesn't bother him. He likes falling asleep against the smell of her neck. Her body is softer. She's not pretty anymore, not by a long shot. But she's still got his number.

So why is he still up? He thought he was reading through documents, preparing for a meeting with the foundation. Microloans in scorned countries once enslaved by enemies. But he hasn't looked at his papers for an hour. This is unusual for him. A little alone time. A little thinking. Time thinking is not time working, not time learning, not time next to his wife, not time on the phone with his daughter. Time costs. Time is.

It's a gibbous moon, three quarters full. He can't see across the green landscape of his tiny little estate. It wasn't cheap, this place. History or not. The house was on the wrong side of a war, a good reminder both of cycles and of progress. He doesn't believe in ghosts. He doesn't even believe in history the way many people do. He believes in systems, data, and character. See the facts, no matter what they may be. There's always one more question. Make the best decisions you can. Go with it. Recognize your people. Don't be too hard on yourself. Climb, conserve, confess. Forgive. That takes time too. All your time, perhaps.

There are two dogs out there, a security guard, and cameras everywhere. In the trees, on the dock, in the birdhouse at the foot of the drive. It's not an easy house to get to. Protected. Water on two sides. It's all out there.

Yet here they come, the men at night. Three ships drifting silently like ducks over the placid waters. The men wear black and the boats are black. Small things with paddles. There are three passengers in each. He can't see them. It's all too far away. There should be dogs barking. But there are no dogs tonight.

He hears something. What? Something. He stands and turns toward the refrigerator. Time to go upstairs, slide next to his wife. Maybe he won't wash his face, brush his teeth. He'll just pull right next to her.

The man in front of him wears black sleeves, black socks, a thin wetsuit, a slick mask over the mouth and eyes. The man raises a finger to where the lips should be. There's a half-second to find something heavy, something sharp, but instead he just spreads his hands apart. Then there are many men in the room.

"Listen," he begins, but he's interrupted. He can't tell which of the men is talking.

"You have a wife upstairs. Forty-five minutes ago she took three milligrams of Lunesta. She's wearing a white nightdress. If you say another word she'll be shot in the head."

His arms are gripped from behind. His mouth opens, but before anything comes out his head is hooded and wrapped in tape. His clothes are cut from him. He feels the needle. He feels something pressed into his asshole. He feels the thick diapers wrapping his waist. And then nothing.

4

He's inside a room. The handcuffs have been loosened and connected with a brushed steel chain that keeps him seated. His feet are chained together, too. They've taken the cloth hood. He doesn't know how long it was on the boat—an hour, twenty minutes. Then lifted by four sets of hands, carried a short distance swiftly. There's nothing special about this room. He's on a firm sofa with a paisley print that agrees with the floral wallpaper. His wife would notice that. There's also an overstuffed chair, a thin rubber mat on the floor, and a window covered in heavy-duty masking tape. He's wearing grey athletic shorts and a yellow t-shirt. His feet are socks. Outside there are crickets.

It's his first time in handcuffs, let alone ankle chains, but his body understands immediately. His limbs have developed alternative planes of balance and movement. His facility for adaptation has always been under-rated. She knows. His wrestling buddies know. He leans forward, rests his wrists on his hip, spreads his knees and elbows out, and waits for the door to open.

She must be safe. This world was never discussed out of his duty to her. Except duty without strength is a dereliction. What good is recognizing the right thing to do if you're powerless? Look at him. If there's anyone who questions the practice of strength first and duty second—well just look at him.

But there are many kinds of strength, he must remember. Just because they have him does not mean they're stronger. Who? An enemy. So many. Zealots, crazies, hippies, bullies stabbed in bureaucratic knife fights. He's been stabbed, too. But there are friends. Who doesn't he know that's worth knowing? Yet he doesn't know this situation. Not yet.

He can hear people walking past the door but maybe an hour passes before anyone comes in. The man who enters is not young, not as old as him, but not as healthy, either. He is seventy-six, this man is barely sixty. White-haired, stooped, a mid-level civil servant. He's met lots of men like this. They're smart enough, but they lack ambition. Maybe they had ambition once when they were twenty, but then they had children, took out loans, they lost their sleep and edge. Fat and happy yet beaten down, all at the same time. Tangled in their anchor chain. The man is poorly dressed except for a beautiful tie. An old-world bureaucrat, he thinks. I'm going to survive.

The man sits on the chair in front of him, a clipboard on his lap with regular A4 paper. Twitchy. It takes considerable willpower to wait for the man to speak first, but he waits. He synchs his breathing up and holds the man's eyes firmly. Although what he would like to do is rip them from their sockets and pop the jelly out.

"What's your name?" the man asks.

"Donald," he says. "What's yours?" The man hesitates ever so slightly, squinting as if he's forgotten his glasses. And perhaps he has. The glasses are sitting on his marble kitchen island where a woman is prepping celery and carrots for a stew. Is she worrying a little bit about how forgetful her husband has become? She should be worried, because it looks like honey bunch may not clear hurdle number one. The man's hand is creeping toward his forehead. When it gets there, when it rests there for a moment, the man will rub his glassless eyes and nose and lips and the prisoner will take over. But the man stops himself. The training and experience holds. Wife shouldn't worry. He has the tie, she's done her part. The man's stooped face squares its edges again like a manly watch case. "It's better that you don't know," the man says.

"Better in what sense?"

"In that you need to cooperate," the man says.

"Fine. Let's try that."

The man writes down his name, age, address, date and place of birth. The man could be a border guard, someone who checks hundreds of passports a day, asking a few simple questions to each traveler before sliding their documents back and waving them into the country.

"Have you traveled much?"

"Yes," he says. "Yourself?"

The man puts his pen down. He's going to punch me, Donald thinks. No, he isn't. There, right there is the difference. He knows everything there is to know about this man. He knows where he left his glasses and ambition and what his wife is making for dinner and where she bought his tie. He knows that he used to smoke. He knows everything but what good does it do him?

"What is going on here?" he intones. He's surprised by the menace in his voice. Is he more angry than he knew? Of course he is. And less frightened, too. He's an old man, kidnapped from his house. His wife has been threatened. "You don't look like a kidnapper." Never move your head when you give an order.

"I'm not the person you ask questions to," the man responds. "I'm not here for that." The man strokes his clipboard, as if making invisible ink appear. Then he flips up the page and points to a familiar map—hello!— that Donald spent years staring at, watching coded colors shift. The man points to the worst corner, where dark sludge oozed incessantly through seams. "You were in the mountains seven years ago."

"That's true. Also eight, six, five, four, and three years ago."

The man makes some notes on his form. "What were you doing there?"

"There's a war going on." He waits for some recognition from the man. "I was working for the government." His left wrist begins to bleed, except it doesn't. He swaps the top for the bottom. He can see from the man's face that, for a moment, the man forgot he was in chains.

"Which government?"

"Our government."

"Any others?"

"No. No others. Only ours. And my office had something to do with that war, which you probably know, presuming you watch the news. Presuming you know anything. I was there a lot. I was there all the time. You probably know exactly why I was there, which is why you know I was there at all. It's not a big secret."

"How about you just presume I don't know anything."

"Because then you would be an idiot. I can presume that if you want."

The man blinks and looks away. The man stands up. Shuffling one sheet of paper under another. "I'm not your enemy," he says.

"I know you're not." If the man will just look at him again, he can reach inside the man's chest and tease out that long white string of obedience. He's spent his whole life taking a wire brush to bureaucrats like this. "You're being forced into a position you shouldn't be in. There's still time. You either fix something like this swiftly or it gets out of control fast."

The man's nose itches, but he fights it. He fights and he wins. The man is getting stronger. He's more capable than he looks. "I'm going to tell you something for your own good," the man says. "You should know. The next person asking you questions. You should consider answering them with a little less commentary. It's in your interest."

He makes a quick decision. "That's a beautiful tie," he says. And when the head reflexively tilts to look, he leaps up and jumps at the man.

But he's miscalculated. The couch keeps him stuck. He doesn't feel anything except the sensation of being stuck. Stuck and a pain in his shoulder, the one he separated, long ago, an old wrestling injury that kept him from greatness. He pulls on his shackles. He strains and somehow keeps his balance. "You cocksucker," he snarls. The man, barely sixty and plenty years his junior, looks to the door, waits a moment to see if anybody is coming in. But nobody comes. The man turns back to him, taps him on the shoulder, and then smacks him lightly on the cheek.

Hands on his chest, feet together: he sleeps like this.

In the morning a young man comes in dressed as a prison guard. The young guard is healthy looking, his short sleeves pressed, the kind of boy he likes: neat, obedient, squared away. When you're old you can go to work in your corduroys, but you have to earn it. The young guard removes the chains and shackles and watches him pace the room and swing his arms.

"Pretty country out here, isn't it?" Donald says. The guard is not his enemy. The guard, in fact, is going to be his friend.

"Do you need to use the facilities?" the guard says.

He catches a glimpse of himself in the guard's mirrored sunglasses. "Thank you, soldier."

The guard shows him a bathroom just through the open door. The tile is newly grouted, the wallpaper vines and cherries. Then, to his surprise, the guard leaves. There's no window in the bathroom. In the mirror he recognizes himself again, although his face looks tired. His eyes are triple underlined with wrinkles cut halfway to bone. Of course he's tired. There's nothing in the bathroom cabinet except for faint brown rings where bottles sat not long ago. The tub and underneath the sink have both been cleared out too. The curtain rod is plastic and the metal piping's tight. When he emerges the young guard is waiting for him.

"My goodness," he says to the guard. "I guess I really pissed somebody off, now, didn't I?"

The guard doesn't answer and sternly looks him back into the room. There's a cup of tea and some fried bread wrapped in a paper towel on the floor beside the couch. The guard closes the door. If he's to be reshackled, it's not this time. I need something to write with, he thinks. He begins to search the room.

Every three or four hours a different guard comes with food. Every three or four hours he goes to the bathroom. In the meantime he makes mental lists. He lists the guards in order of which look most vulnerable to ambush. He lists the possible locations this could be. He lists the different groups, factions, and individuals that may be behind this. He lists the people who might be most able to help him. He lists his other assets, but they seem few. The room is empty. There's nothing of use.

When the young guard cycles back through Donald asks him about a regional sports event he recalls was set to take place last night.

"We won," says the young guard.

"Close?" he says.

The young guard nods noncommittally. He seems to regret speaking. But then he says, "Look, I don't know what you've done or why they want you so badly."

"You're doing your job." If you get the objectives right, the lieutenant can write the strategy. But the right lieutenant can also be the one who points out that the objectives are wrong.

"I've seen how your house is," the young guard says nervously. This boy! This boy was there! In his goddamn kitchen! "And your family. You don't seem like the kind of person to cause any trouble."

"That's good judgment. But you also have a job to do. The only thing I'd ask right now is to get me something to write with and advise my wife that I'm alive." His objective is simple and clear. "Wives—they didn't sign up for this, did they? I don't know how they do it. That's permissible. It's probably on the checklist. Don't let it slip through the cracks."

"There's nothing I can do," the guard says, and closes the door.

*   *   *

He's not far from home. In the region, on the water, within the young guard's "we," with paisley sofas and new tiles. He crosses two locations off his list. Wherever he is, they're not worried about him escaping, which means this is where he should escape. Of course he's not supposed to be here. Heads are going to roll. If anybody should know about this house it's him, but he doesn't. It could be private enterprise, or clandestine, or even covert, or all of them at once, or something renegade, although the insult slap was legal, technically. Open handed, fingers spread apart, initiated from twelve to fourteen inches away. It requires practice. It also requires written permission from the control element chief that doubtfully was given, but could be issued retroactively, if there's such a chief, if anything that should be still is. He wonders who decided he should be unchained. A flaw in the procedure or a reasoned step in his direction? He allocates it to the list of his accomplishments. His conversation with the guard goes on there, too.

Surveying the room again, he discovers that the top inch of the window has been taped on the inside, not the outside. He stands on the edge of the couch and peels the strip off without difficulty. It hasn't been taped for long. Dusk light splashes a thin orange bar against the wall. He can't see much. A slice of grassy yard, another tendril of the house. There's no one out there. The window has been recently screwed shut. The glass is tempered, double-paned, and he decides to work on the screws, first using the edge of the tea-cup. The first screw comes loose but the other ones are sunk well. The cup chips in his thinning, spotted hands. Could you cut a throat with it? What else does the room offer to break serious glass? Then he decides against. He needs more information. Let's see who my little gambit brings out next, he thinks. He lies down on the mat to listen and rest.

Some time later he is escorted by a new guard into a plain dining room with an old but well-kept triple pedestal table. It occurs to him that this is still somebody's house. Somebody lives here and they've loaned their house to these guests, and the guests have taken him captive. Drop cloths have been draped over the paintings on the wall. There are windows in this room and they look out on endless green fields. Nothing but grass for miles. Two more locations off the list.

He's seated at the table, handcuffed through the chair, with plastic flexicuffs on his ankles. After a while two men come into the room and sit across from him. One looks like the first man that questioned him, except his bearing is different. He has better posture and is drinking hot tea. The other is fat with glasses. The fat man sets Donald's wife's purse on the table. Mutt and Jeff.

"Tell us what you were doing in the mountains," the first man says.

"Where did you get that?" He can't stop looking at the purse. He pictures a gun inside it with two bullets.

The fat one slides the purse off the table with one stubby arm, chewing cud. He must be Mutt. Jeff holds up another map, although this one has been blown up and laminated. Gosh, I'm really moving up the chain now, he thinks.

"What were you doing up there?" Jeff asks, pointing with his tea cup.

"Why? Those people were our allies. Am I under arrest? If you're arresting me then I would like a lawyer."

"I thought you *were* a lawyer." Mutt says.

"No," he replies. "I never finished law school. So maybe you don't know everything?"

"Or maybe you lied on a resume at some point."

"Not likely."

"Listen," Jeff says. "We can't help you with the lawyer thing. It's not that kind of deal. The deal is the kind of thing that can get a lot worse. Look at this place. This is a house. If you don't cooperate, or maybe even if you do cooperate, the next place will not be a house."

"Where is your passport?" Mutt asks.

"Safe."

The men exchange a meaty look. The fat man shakes his head and almost smiles, chop-crossing his hands through the air like an umpire. "Saaaafe!" Jeff waves his colleague off with one limp flirtatious hand. "Tell us about this trip."

"Where is my wife?" he asks. "What have you done to her?"

"We're not at liberty to say," Mutt explains.

"Can't help you there," Jeff says. "I'm not a social worker."

"What would you say you were?"

"Look around you," Jeff says. "It's nice here. This whole thing can get incredibly unpleasant."

"I'm just establishing that my wife is not relevant."

"To what?"

"To this." He tries to gesticulate but he's cuffed. He's still got his head and shoulders, but without hands it's tough.

Jeff squints at him and tousles the little white string of tea bag with one finger. "This what?" Jeff leans forward. A great truth is about to be revealed. "This this. This!"

"Which this is that?" Mutt's leaning, too.

Has he said something? What are they about to know? "Are you kidding me? Kidnapped! Chains, goddamn it! You!"

The two men gaze at one another. "Or maybe you?" the fat man says, gaping his mouth wide as if he's trying to clear his ears.

"We're definitely not kidding," says Jeff.

"I'm not saying a blessed thing unless my wife's okay."

"We're not here for that."

"Well that's been established," he says. "But consider. First: you want information from me concerning legitimate activity. Second: you've proposed that my treatment depends on my cooperation. Third: you've *implied* that my wife's treatment depends on my cooperation. Yet you have not even asked me to cooperate specifically. Does that make any sense? Is that good judgment?" He's got his right hand working, shackles and all, turning an imaginary dial in the air. "You're going to have a dickens of a time unless you separate that which is separate." It's the new regime. That's who it is. The kid from the library. The commission. An old grudge or two. They're all on the list. Some newly powerful asshole has called for his head and some bony jerk has helped them. Here he is.

"A reasonable effort will be made," says the first man. "Now let's return to the mountains."

He knows exactly what they're doing but it still takes every ounce of his soul to restrain himself. He used to snow mad flurries of five-line memos down on idiots like these. This is going to cost them everything. Too bad they don't have much. "You bet," he says. "When you give me your word." His eyes are on Jeff. He went to school with morons like this. Breezy. Everything comes easy. Not a scholarship kid. Not a student soldier. Not by a long shot. He looks forward to ruining his life.

"You got it," Jeff says.

For the next hour he explains his trips, the people he met with, the reasons for his visits. He wants to run his hands over his face but can't, so instead he closes his eyes and stares briefly at a poster of patience on the inside of his lids. He speaks slowly and does not waste words. Organized. Bullet points. They seem interested. Impressed? They listen. There were some talks, of course, that he's not permitted to divulge, but these men don't seem to know about them, or have any interest in them. They don't really seem to know anything. All they have are detailed travel records. They corroborate airports, customs data, itineraries, dates. He imagines sweeps across the country, hundreds of thousands of people pulled from their beds, shackled, thrown in the backs of trucks, driven to secret locations, and asked what they had been doing in those goddamn mountains.

"Check everything," he tells the men. He feels incredibly calm. "It's all true." Fifty invitations a week and now look at him!

It seems like they're thinking and then Jeff says, "Pretty out here." In unison, they all gaze out the window at the fields, long and green and flat. "Yeah," the fat man says, winking at his partner. "Feels like getting away from it all, doesn't it?"

"For sure," Jeff says.

"Be nice to have a little place," says Mutt.

"Uh-huh." Jeff walks over to the window presses a hand against the glass.

"Yeah, right?"

"And so close to the city," Donald tosses in. That snaps them out of it. But he's right! He's still close! He needs to get back to the room. He can break the window. He can escape. "I was paid to serve the people. Is a man's word still worth something, way out here?" he says. "Is it? Check my references. Check everything."

The fat man stands up and starts strolling down one side of the table, dragging one finger along as if testing for dust.

"Now hold on," Jeff calls out. "Just you hold on!" Jeff puts his tea down with a clank. A sluice of liquid eases over the side, turning the tea bag paper dark. The fat man stops, leaning on five fingertips. From a back pocket Mutt withdraws a set of handcuffs.

"Do you know where I got these?"

"I do not."

"The wife of a dead man gave me these." Mutt flicks the cuffs open and locks them on Donald's wrist right next to the flexicuffs already on him. "Lot of blood's on your hands."

"That's just false." He keeps his eyes on Jeff. "Tell your boss I'm here. Tell his boss. Tell it until there aren't any bosses left. You won't be sorry you did. They want to know. For darn sure. You have something very valuable."

The two men mind-meld. They seem less stupid with their mouths shut, as they access their small, shared brain in stasis. "Time!" Jeff calls out into the empty house, and his voice bounces away like a tiny rubber ball.

* * *

He is escorted back to his room by two guards. One guard removes the flexicuffs, but it takes him a while because he's using a pair of scissors. The other guard asks if he needs to use the facilities. Then the young guard comes with food. "My wife," he tells the young guard. "Please have someone get in touch with her." He smiles sadly. "She'll think I ran off with a tart." But the young guard gums his lips.

When the young guard leaves he tips over the couch and unscrews one of its stubby legs. Things are not going well enough or fast enough. He's close. Just down the river, a few clicks from his buddy's house, he's sure. He coughs loudly and stabs the corner of the window with the couch leg as hard as he can. It doesn't break. Before he can try again all three guards run into the room. They push him down on his stomach, shackle his hands and feet, put the couch back together, and chain him to it. They've been watching him! The young guard squats and screws the couch to the wall with a cordless drill, his face even for a moment with Donald's.

"Well what would you have done?" Donald asks him.

He tries to yank the couch apart. He does it gently at first so that they'll think it's futile, but even when he yanks in earnest there's no progress. His lists are shot.

At night he is brought back to the dining room. This time the door to the kitchen is propped open, and inside he sees a barefoot shirtless man in beige dress pants sitting on a stool with a black hood on his head. Mutt and Jeff stand on either side of the stool, arguing about something. The fat man holds a brown leather belt. Jeff is drinking hot tea. And there's someone else in there with them, someone with a foreign accent. Then the kitchen door swings shut and he is handcuffed and seated at the table with the kitchen door behind him.

After a while the two men emerge from the kitchen. He has planned a little speech but their nose breathing stops him. The fat man's taken his jacket off, shirtsleeves rolled up above the elbow. Jeff is drinking a diet soda. The silver oval of the pop top brims with sharpness.

"You hungry?" Jeff says.

"What did you find out?"

"We need to hear more."

"I've told you everything."

"We've released people in the past," says Jeff.

"The dates," says Mutt.

"Things will go better, things could go really well." Jeff finishes his drink and looks around for somewhere to put it. "I've seen it before." He places the can on the mantle and it rolls and black liquid dribbles out. "I think we are coming to a conclusion for you."

He wants to ask about the hooded man in the kitchen. But where will that get him? Instead he says, "I'll tell you whatever you want. I'll go over it as many times as need be. But let me make something clear."

"Oh it's clear." Mutt digs out something in his eye, flicking it off his thumb like a spark. "Marriage," the fat man says, ambling down the table toward him. "Love. And. Marriage. Love— "

"It seems you've got another chance," Jeff jumps in. "How often does anyone get that? All you have to do is cooperate. We are coming to a conclusion, but you absolutely must cooperate."

"Tell us about Tuesday." Mutt's behind him. He tenses up his neck for the strike, but it doesn't come. I could take these guys, he thinks. I'm ancient and I could take them. How does the trapped wolf that chews its own leg off weigh survival against revenge?

"You bet," he says. "Let's run through it again."

And while he is talking about a village and a restaurant where he ate with the head of a foreign petrochemical corporation, Mutt reaches into his pocket and pulls out a phone. The fat man motions for Donald to keep talking as Mutt stands up, saying to someone on the other line, "We've got one for you."

That night, lying on the mat, he hears a banging noise in the next room and then a series of dull thuds like a heavy bag hit with a bat. After that he does not sleep. His ankle is cuffed to an old steam radiator, which he tries to tear out of the floor, but it's not going anywhere. In the morning six men come into the room, wrap shackles around his waist, and attach his handcuffs to the shackles so he has to walk bent over. They run another chain from his waist to his leg shackles. Then they cover his ears in giant headphones and hood him and wrap tape around the top third of his head. He feels the needle. He feels something pressed into his anus. He feels the thick diapers wrapping his waist. Then they take him away.

5

The plane bounces once, twice, hard, and then again. His legs itch. A DVT seems possible. He wonders what kind of paperwork would happen if a clot blows up his heart. He is cold. He's been cold a long time. He wants an old sweater, the grey one with the collar. There are men next to him and across from him and behind him. They can't see either. A flash penetrates his hood. Lightning! The men smell like hair rotting in a drain. Everyone's chained together like one big criminal family. A line of soldiers sits facing them, knives unsheathed, beaded up. Cameras, not lightning. The fat plane taxies along on a Sunday drive. The pilot's a plumber, nugget, Whiskey Delta. When they finally stop he realizes how hungry he is. Half starving, half sleeping, half drugged, half everything.

"Where are we?" he calls out.

Something metal strikes his shoulder. "Shut up, motherfucker," a voice says. "If you speak again I'll kill you."

He nods. Well of course this was going to be difficult. Transitions bring out the worst.

They walk him down the ramp at the back of the plane. The metal is cold and slippery against his stocking feet. He's not someone who minds the cold, but this is cold that sends you back inside with the paper to put a kettle on to boil. He struggles to stay upright. His shoulders shake. He can't be that cold, can he? The socks do make it easier to shuffle with the shackles on, but his feet are getting wet. It's unpleasant. He can't remember which socks they are. He hasn't bought socks in a while. His wife no longer shops for him, something he approves of as a change of life. An assumption of the less momentous tasks of the world—not critical but still necessary, and perhaps fulfilling in their minor way. Charm the pretty clerk in men's hosiery. Count your own change, save your receipt. His hood sucks in and out, and he tries to keep pulling the air in slowly through his nose and angling it down and out again when he pushes it out of his mouth, but he needs more air than that. Walking in a hood is not the same as sitting in one. He sucks in a breath and the hood clings to his mouth. So he presses his teeth against his lip and tries drawing in air from the corners of his mouth. The hood simply pulls in completely and even slips into his mouth for a moment, tasting a little bit of garlic. It's disgusting. He spits it out. He breathes and spits and breathes until he's sure they'll notice. His hood is beating like a heart. He was once able to hold his breath for two full minutes but look at him.

"Air," he whispers before he can stop. "Can I please get some air?" He doesn't want to be that guy, but here he is, that guy. A hand pulls the hood back above his mouth and he takes a deep breath. "Thank you," he gasps.

"Don't thank me, motherfucker." The hood yanks down again.

He stumbles in the mud. His escorts tighten their grip. They drag him toward a cloud of sound big enough to worm through earmuffs. The mud feels like a clue, but he has a feeling that solving it lacks significance. Later he will realize exactly where they are, but for now he still can't think. The atmosphere is thin and cheap. A low-rent part of the world. The hood is still disgusting, but there's one angle with his head that squirts freshness in thin tendrils to his mouth. Give him time and he will master hood-wearing as well. He's always been a quick learner. The bodies around him are jerky and smell like leeks and batteries. And they are not behaving well. A sleeve rasps against his knuckles and he reaches for it, feels a roughness in the cloth that frightens him. He tries to hold on but the sleeve leaves him as he begins to fall. A dozen knees pin him prone to the ground, knees on his legs, ankles, head, back. The shackles come off and a cold sharp metal line creeps up his leg. They're cutting off his clothes. The cold air washes across his skin. The fabric vanishes, the shackles and cuffs leap back on. Naked. In chains. Then a hand yanks off his hood and flips off his goggles and his earmuffs.

The roar of the world is fire, a long explosion of yellow light and grinding asteroids. He tries to unsquint but the soldier is there, holding his hood up like he's adding a flourish to a magic trick. The soldier has dark skin and wears oversized aviator glasses that should make his big nose look smaller but don't. There's a bright flash as someone snaps his picture—their wedding photo, his retirement party, his arm around a stranger, around a solider just like this one—and then the hood is back again and the world is dark or darkish, but not before he's seen men.

There are men in drab slacks and tunics, men in uniform, men with half-fez-half-beanies and combat helmets. There are infantry with guns, mountain men, city men, warrior men, office men, men everywhere under bright klieg lights, and K-9s barking in a chorus line behind balled-up concertina in the cold bedpan desert with airless mountains slashed in an angry hand across the horizon. There are men lying on the ground like sticks with men stomping on their backs in front of low buildings on a purple moon. It is a world of single-minded men and order. He has been here before. He has been many places of such purpose, but none was the same. He closes his eyes beneath the hood and listens to the machinery slaughter until he can pick out the parts: Lawn Dart engines, twenty-year-old field generators, screaming in the mountain tongues, hometown dogs. He's in a crowd now. It's been a long time since he's been uncontrollably in a crowd, and despite the madness there's something comforting. He breathes slowly through his nose in his hood mashed up next to strangers. It's hard to be calm in a vacuum, but he could always be calmer than someone else. He can't tell if the other prisoners are chained too, as they seem to be moving better than he is, but that could just be age. Fear up. This kind of thing is for the young.

His hood is not the top of the line, for without the goggles he can see something through it, enough at least to know that they are moving inside, narrowing to a kind of single line. When exactly his escorts from the plane stopped accompanying him he cannot say. He's calming down and down. The crowd is scared shitless and screaming crying raving mad, but in their panic he feels a separation from them. Back in the house he was the only one who understood his situation, but here, in this context, any God or satellite can look down and data mine him from the crowd.

They're being herded through a cattle run and he can hear the locks and gates ahead of him. There will be, he knows, very few opportunities to step outside this process. The interrogator's job is to talk to him, and the soldier's job is to not talk to him, and opportunity, if there is any, lies in finding someone in between looking for a chance to distinguish himself. He used to promote people like that, often. Just one is all he needs right now.

When his hood comes off again he's in a small room with knotty wooden floors and no windows. The walls are plywood and there are six painter's clip lights with energy-saving bulbs. There's a soldier on the in-door and a soldier on the out-door and two soldiers who push him down to the floor. They're yelling at him but mostly they are putting their knees on his lower back and knees and shoulder blades to pin him in place. He tenses up his core to protect himself but keeps everything else half-loose. The conceding wrestler's trick. It's been a long time since he's been pinned like that. Once it was as much a part of his daily life as brushing his teeth. There's cold metal against his calves and they're unshackling him. They are rough but good. You train an army for years for perfection on one day. He stands naked and seventy-six years old in chains and socks with two MPs and two twenty-something reservists from out West or down South in desert fatigues. No ranks visible. No name tags. He knows what their jobs are. He knows what they're doing when they lean him over the table and stick a finger into his rectum. He knows he should not talk to them and he doesn't.

In the next room a barber shaves his head. It's very fast. One day he'll make a joke about it. They take one picture before and one after. He's on the floor again, unshackled, reshackled, a blue jumpsuit applied to his person in between. The collaboration is getting easier. They're all improving. A very blond soldier takes his fingerprints. A mouthswab. His technique's good, although there used to be all kinds of problems with the data. He wonders what Blondie does for a living back home. There's something gentle in the way the man straightens the jumpsuit around him, pulling the slack to fit things right. It would surprise you the different kinds of people who make good soldiers.

"Soldier," he says.

"Shut your mouth," says Blondie. Getting talked to like that makes him feel younger.

"Bag and tag," someone says.

They walk him to an open hall, and there beyond he sees, for the first time, the waves of cells there in the hangar. An impromptu zoo made of great rolls of wire and circus lights. Dogs are barking. He knows that there's a plan but it seems too chaotic, and he wonders if the man who drew it up ever stood right here and watched his vision work. Or if that man sees only blueprints rolled tight in a stiff clean cardboard tube. He once thought the easiest way to send your enemies to hell was raining hell upon your enemies, but it is more complicated than that. First you have to set up hell. Then you have to find your enemies. Then make that meeting happen.

At a small table, a man with a cheap laptop and bulky printer accepts the documents from his escorts, enters the data, and produces two cards with a number on it. It's a pretty high figure. One card disappears into an escort's pocket and the other is inserted into a file. His escort turns him around and he can feel the pen on his back. "Good number," the escort says.

"Yeah," says the man with the laptop. "Huh."

The escorts disappear. Donald is moved into another room made entirely of unfinished sheetrock. There's no door or ceiling. Echoed generators, yelling soldiers, screaming prisoners, dogs. The tall black man and the shorter white one in the room are wearing civilian clothes and caps. The black guy has a good stare. Get pretty far with a stare like that. On the other hand, this fellow hasn't gotten very far because it's still the stare of a henchman, and the only reason to remain a henchman with a stare like that is being too ornery, stupid, or both to overcome.

The henchman walks around him several times, as if appraising his blue suit for style. He finally comes to rest in front of him. The henchman may not be the brightest bulb or sharpest blade, but he understands power. There are men like this on both sides of this war. The henchman may not be able to look each prisoner in the eye and see good or evil, but that's not his job. The henchman's job is strength or weakness.

Donald has spent his whole life earning the respect of men like this. *Tough son of a bitch. Ruthless little bastard.* He's been called these things. There's a handsome gift in his office inscribed with a reminder that victory is never final, defeat is never fatal, and courage is what counts. He looks the soldier in the eye. He sees courage there. He almost reaches for his glasses before he realizes that his hands are cuffed behind his back and his glasses are long gone. No hair, no glasses, no suit, no authority, no range of motion—he is unrecognizable! So he blinks, he nods, and he looks. Look at me! There's some famous footage of him in smoking wreckage, jacket off, sleeves rolled up, tie loose, a decisive hero carrying wounded to safety. Now zoom in. Look at the eyes. Parse the wrinkles. Remember? Know me. Recognize. Even here, personal courage must count for a lot.

The black man's eyes are liquid dark and pour down into him, dissolving into his blood. They circle through his heart, his groin, his legs, his belly. They flow up to his neck and through his head and pull back out his eyeholes. Errors have been made, lies perpetrated, mischief carried out, but this is war. Stuff happens that makes an individual error like his being here difficult to correct. You move on. You try to do better next time. But there *is* a process. There's a system. This system may take some time but its workings start right here, with a henchman trained to recognize the incongruence of pictures and inconsistent data. Once the error is recognized, a series of red flags, queries, and reports begins. It moves from desk to desk until someone has earned a star, someone a court-martial, and a boatful of people enormous belly laughs. And one day I'll laugh too at how someone tried to rewire this system for revenge. Who? How grim? How high?

The black man's taking in air, chest bellowing up for some kind of blast. "When's the last time you saw him?" the henchman barks. He's holding up a picture of a long-faced, handsome man, bearded, with bright, intelligent eyes. He's tall, too, although the picture might not say so, but everyone knows because this is the most famous man in the world. "When! Tell me! Now!"

6

They give him some old shoes and a cap and then five guards shuffle him into a windowless old barn of corrugated sheet steel. There's no floor. The makeshift cells are shaped from concertina wire. At either end of the barn stands an armed overwatch in a makeshift mini-tower with a light machine gun. His cell is in the far corner. There's no door. One guard uses heavy gloves to pull away the wire. Another guard stands back with a drawn pistol. The overwatch train their weapons on him, too. They push him into the cell and lie him on his belly in the dirt, legs crossed and bent at the knees, hands crossed behind his head. Three guards unshackle him. It takes some time. How could he have ever thought this fighting force could be light and lethal? When they are done, they back up and hurry from him as from a pyre of burning slag, pulling the wire back shut. He rises to his feet.

"Don't touch the wire," the last guard says.

"Is it electric?" He knows it's not.

"Just don't touch it," the guard says.

There's nothing in there but two blankets, a shawl, a bucket, and a plastic water bottle. He tries to peer through the bullet holes in the outside walls, but without his glasses he can't see much. Generators thrum the air. Voices are speaking his language but also others. Something's burning, somewhere close. There's the sound of a game going on outside, maybe a soldiers' barbeque. He can see the cell beside his, but the ones in front of him are blocked with sheet metal. The man in the neighboring cell squats over his bucket, and he looks away.

Later in the day a skinny soldier comes by and tosses something over the wire. The military rations have changed since he was a pilot, but not so much that he can't see that these are modified: no pepper, no chocolate, no water heater, no spoon. You have to tear them open with your teeth, although his neighbor uses the wire. He folds up a bit of cardboard from the pack as a utensil. The food is not good but the nutritional information on the package is reassuring and interesting. One thing he knows about this place is that they won't permit you to starve. Unpleasant things do happen. Starvation is not one of them. He finishes quickly and then watches his neighbor eating beans more slowly, muttering to himself in a weird guttural bird tongue. It must be less than ten minutes before the skinny soldier comes back down the line, half-singing like a street vendor. "Trash! Trashy, trashy, trash, here!" He remembers the duck from the restaurant, the dark meat slipping off the bone, shiny with fat. He slides his hand-compacted trash out through the wire and the soldier pokes through it to make sure that everything's there. It is. The skinny soldier looks him up and down and nods. He moves the skinny soldier to the top of his list.

He walks around and around his cell. Because he is at the end of the row, he can only see his one neighbor, the man with a faded scar on his chin. His neighbor sits crosslegged, flexible and still, quietly reading a book.

He checks the overwatch but they don't seem especially attentive. From the edge of the wire, he whispers a foreign greeting at his neighbor. The man looks up.

"Where can I get one of those?" he asks the man, pointing to the book. The man puts his head down and continues reading.

*   *   *

Outside, through the bullet holes, he can make out wooden platform tents laid out in orderly rows, with canvas roofs and open sides, surrounded by double rows of concertina wire. Ten to twenty prisoners in each tent. One bucket. He would rather be out there with them except for the communal bucket. Still, the next time the skinny soldier comes by with the meals, he calls out to him.

"Can I please go outside?"

"That's general population," the thin soldier says. "Can't help you."

As if on cue, a wave of human sound ripples in from outside, and his neighbor next door kneels down on his mat.

"Not the praying kind?" the soldier says. "You're better off in the barn."

"I'm high value," he calls out. "I have time-sensitive intel."

The soldier laughs and strolls on. "Who's the crazy new-Bob?" the soldier calls to the overwatch, but the overwatch only wags a steel muzzle in answer.

He doesn't know how long he's been asleep before he's woken by soldiers yelling and rattling the wire. "On your knees!" they're shouting. "On your knees!" The barn is floodlit from both ends as if a high-octane sports contest is set to commence. He creaks to his knees and the soldiers rush in, cuff his hands, push him flat, chain his legs and hood him. The skinny solider isn't there. He can hear the wind bellowing outside, hurling sand against the barn. He's dragged an unknowable distance before he's pressed into a chair and unhooded. Progress, he thinks.

It's a concrete cell block with a small window boarded up and a faded carpet, once red and grey and beige. There's a small wooden table and two cheap plastic chairs. Two guards stand against the wall and a man in civilian's clothes sits on the other side of the table. His white shirt is barely wrinkled. His hair is combed and sprayed tight. He's in his mid-late-twenties and looks ethnic.

"Please state your name," says the man in a voice flat and bland as pudding.

He doesn't answer right away, spreading his knees and elbows out as far as the chains will let him. He used to wake up quickly. He still does. But they don't know that, do they? He blinks and squints and yawns, giving everyone time. The interrogator is not in uniform but he should be. He's too young, wears boots, still has the multipurpose knife on his belt. He belongs to the armies. Among the agencies with interests in Donald's future the armies may be the best disposed, although he made enemies there, too. He synchs up his breathing the best he can and states his name, appending the last title he held when he retired from government. "Ex," he adds.

"Ex," the man repeats. His expression makes it hard to tell if he just looks like that or is smiling. "My name is Jolman."

A name. It floats between them like an orange lifebuoy. "I appreciate that, Jolman."

Jolman nods. "I am going to need a lot of information from you today and over the next few…" Jolman shrugs the missing word off into the air.

"And I'm going to help you, Jolman." He states his number, address, age. "I've been married fifty-five years. I've served in government most of my life, as you must know, government and then business when the wind was blowing the other way." It's almost cordial, two strangers getting to know one another in a small coincidental moment. "I've been very fortunate. Present environs notwithstanding."

"Children?"

He hesitates. Not because he is going to lie about his children. But it occurs to him that if they are going to change direction they should do it now. Don't wait until you're talking about some petrochemical asshole in the mountains. Now.

"Jolman." He tries to imagine he's on the phone. Jolman can't see me. He can only hear my voice. "Let me just say that when we're finished here today, you'll know everything I know about whatever you want to know.

That's a promise. I don't make them often. I've learned my lesson." He lets in a small silence, but not enough to let the man back in yet. "Jolman, let's start by saying I've talked to several folks since this situation began. They have all, if you'll pardon my French, had their heads up their ass. Their access was clearly none. Their scope minute. I am extremely glad you showed up. And I have no intention of insulting your intelligence or your charge here." The words roll through him on simple slides, one idea for each, five slides max. He leans back in his chair as much as circumstance permits. "I know that every scumbag out there comes in here crying *I'm innocent, I've done nothing, I don't know anything!* I'm not saying that. Far from it. From certain standpoints, maybe your own, I'm probably guilty of all kinds of mistakes. I've made plenty, in every part of my life. Did. I disband their army too quickly? Did I run a bad campaign? You bet. And insulted the innocent. Trusted bad lieutenants." He nods his head at the world they share. "I operate at that level, Mr. Jolman. You've got yourself a big fish. And you must move swiftly and with care. Yet." Has he thought this through? All the way to the end? "There's something wrong with this picture, isn't there? You've seen me before. You know my name. You've seen this face." He wants to use his hands, as if his hands would make him recognizable, and maybe they would? "On the wall, in the paper, on the screen. Now add rimless glasses. And some hair—not much, but hair. A dark suit with squared-off shoulders. There's a podium. A flag." Context is everything. "The circle of our country's seal behind me. Line a bunch of vultures from the press up in front of me either eating manure or pecking my eyes out. See the back of their heads? Hell, you already know. But what does it mean? Who turned *that* into *this*? Who's in favor? Who's opposed?" In his mind's eye, shadows are picking sides. The kid from the library. An old friend on the court. The jilted general, the loyal advisor still toiling deep in the machine. "A one-line memo is all it takes. Hell, I'll write it for you. They don't know I'm here. And that means you have the very definition of actionable intel. It's not what they sent you here to find. But it's actionable.

Big time." They're not on the phone. They're looking at each other. They're sitting close.

"Children?" Jolman says.

"Children."

"Do you have children?"

He feels his throat pulse. He hopes it doesn't show. But he knows it does. "Of course I have children." How could he not have children? The body is the mind. His throat beats like a lizard's. He knows what Jolman is trained to do.

"Age and sex of children?"

"All grown up. Two daughters and a son." Patience has never been his virtue and frankly he has gotten worse at it but sometimes patience is the only hammer you have. If you can't move up, move sideways. But move.

"And you? Kids?"

Jolman frowns in a not entirely unfriendly way. "Names?" Jolman writes down their names. "Addresses?"

"I don't know offhand, Jolman." He is getting angry. This thing is bigger than it should be. Conspirators on all sides dreamed this up for him. Some want to turn tables. Some want to make him pay. Some want to torture him, no doubt. Perhaps this is their compromise: turn the tables, make him pay, and then?

"A street name."

"Jolman." He leans forward and a guard steps forward and palms his shoulder back into the chair. But he doesn't even look at the guard. "There's a war going on, Jolman. People are dying. People are doing vicious things. It's more than a war. It's one-point-five generations bent on our destruction. You and I are on one side. The bad guys out there are on all the other ones. They're out there killing us. They won't stop until we stop them. You know that. I know that. At any cost. Am I part of that cost? Please explain. Can I be of service to you via the street names of my children? What am I doing for you? Someone wants to see me suffer, fine, and those may even be your orders, I don't know. My advice," he says, and instantly regrets it, "the record suggests that someone is playing a dangerous game here and hasn't let you in. Don't play the game. At least find out the rules of the game you don't even know you're playing. But please, don't waste time when the real bad guys are outside ready to break." There are famous pictures of the games rogue soldiers have played, pictures that were responsible for the worst day at work he ever had. It felt like someone had hit him the stomach with a bat. He wrote two letters of resignation that week. He experienced a new fear. What other process stuck in the last century was still out there? And sure enough, they came. There are snapshots in his mind of other games few ever saw—between the services, between the branches, between the powers. Things that his buddy somehow managed to get destroyed despite the fact that this century keeps few secrets. Is that what this about? A man like Jolman may never know how hard it is to protect armies from themselves or how flimsy and difficult civilian control really is. A man like Jolman, unless he rises quickly and far, will never know how many enemies you make like that. In the armies, the government, the populace. If you try to please everybody, somebody's not going to like it. If no one hates you, you're not doing much. "Games will lose this war for us, Jolman, if we let them. Games and grudges. Don't let us become our worst enemy. It's so easy. If you only believe one thing I say, please believe that." He scoots toward the table and the guard palms his shoulder again. "Hook me up to a lie detector. Enhance this process however you're going to." He finds Jolman's eyes to make sure they both know what's being said. "Find the truth fast but don't waste time and don't play games because the only way they can destroy us is if we give them lots of help."

Jolman sits quietly across the table, his smooth hands folded patiently in front of him, barely a line or blemish or hair. Wherever his people are from, skin doesn't wrinkle or crack. Jolman has been awake for hours. Showered, shat, and shaved, cut his nails, read the files, run through sequences and scenarios. Jolman is looking at what was once a powerful man, a man respected and even feared, but Jolman does not waver. My goodness, Donald thinks, we do train these boys well.

"You are in a lot of trouble," Jolman says.

"Clearly."

"We have information."

"Then use it. Or just go ahead and torture me, if that's what the sick hippies want. Do what you're gonna do. Get their sick revenge. That's what this is, right?" He's bellowing. There's no sign of backup. "If they dare. Go ahead."

Jolman licks his lips. Jolman shows his first sign of humanity, an emotion that might be anger or might be worry or sadness pulsing between the corners of his railroad mouth. He opens the folder on the desk in front of him, glances at the paper there, then closes it again. "Street name?" Jolman says.

After the interrogation they take him to a new cell. It might be the same day, it might be the next. Hours and hours and hours. Jolman must be tired too. The new cell is in an aircraft hangar, or maybe an old factory, an immense space littered with huge pieces of abandoned machinery frozen in their final act. The machines are labeled with dire warnings, unreadable in the alphabet of another enemy, the good old bad guys of his youth. Old bad guys, new bad guys, each with their own alphabet. The next bad guys don't even have an alphabet! It's impossible to imagine what they once built here. From ground level the sense of space is more massive. Temporary walls and partitions render each section into a thriving neighborhood of cages. The lights are incredibly bright.

There are six cells in his neighborhood. The cells are twelve-foot cages separated by rolls of concertina wire, each with an airlock-style entrance: a rough door made from metal strips, followed by a corridor of four feet, then an identical door that leads into the cell. The floors down here are wooden, some bad-guy wood he doesn't recognize. He's run through the airlock and into the cell.

"Aren't you going to unshackle me?" he asks the guards.

"No."

He stutter-steps into a corner and arranges the two blankets he's been given, rolling one up into a pillow and wrapping himself up in the other. The five other men in there do not look at him or speak to him. He doesn't blame them. There's time.

He knows where he is. He's seen this section of the base on a blueprint and seen other parts firsthand. Within half a mile of this cell is a structure that houses a food court, a movie theater, and some athletic facilities for basketball, volleyball, and workouts. Within a mile of this cell is a command-and-control unit. Within a mile and half is a state university extension where soldiers can continue their coursework. Within two miles there's a line of little orange huts with corrugated metal roofs where soldiers sleep. Around the perimeter lie sandbags big as washing machines. Within a hundred miles, the son of the one-legged man on horseback oils his father's rifle high in the snowy crags, eager for a fight. The power has gone but he still knows everything. That must be worth something.

The main rules are stay away from the wire and don't talk to other prisoners, but even here everyone knows that the breaking is the rule. At the wire's edge he can again make out tiny shards of the outside world where he sees the open tents and prisoners. He stands near the wire all day watching them. He's not sure why. He can hear his cellmates speaking softly to each other, but they do not speak to him.

At night there is no night. The lights stay on. He lies on his blanket for a while and thinks he cannot sleep, until the sound of screaming wakes him up. Recorded screaming and electric guitars and sirens, clangs, gunshots, an infant's cry. The auxiliary talents of this army never cease to astonish him. To his surprise, his cellmates do not seem to move until the guards arrive, banging on the cage and poking through the bars with tiger sticks until everyone's awake. One of his cellmates jumps to his feet defiantly, his arms outstretched for a fight. He's the tallest of the prisoners, with the darkest skin. The tall man glares at him across the room, as if it's all Donald's fault. The tall man's mouth moves silently in prayer or blasphemy, but what jumps out is the familiarity of the lips and tongue and teeth in motion. He's speaking my language, Donald thinks. A colonist.

In the morning there are prayers. The sound rises up over the din of the generators. His cellmates prostrate with their butts in the air like infants on the small thin carpets they all sleep on. They look weak but flexible. It must be good for keeping nimble. He wraps his little shawl around him. He watches them and thumbs through their holy book. The praying men sound mumbly to him but that could be the context. It's never too late to learn, he thinks. Every code was made to be broken. A plan begins to form. Every problem made to be solved. Quitting is easy. His father made sure he understood what was meant by that. You can quit one thing, and then you can quit another, and then pretty soon you're a quitter, defined not by what you've done but by your decisions not to finish what you've started.

By increments, he works his way closer to the colonist, sliding across the concrete a few inches every couple of minutes while the tall man observes without interest. He greets the colonist, who returns the greeting without looking at him.

"How long have you been here?" Donald says. He would like to sit cross-legged too but knows he can't quite manage it. A new goal. The man doesn't answer. "Are there any others like us?" he asks him.

"I'm the only one," the colonist says. He barely moves his lips. "You were questioned last night?"

"Yes."

"They will question you again today. If you do not do well we will all be punished."

"Can you get me one of these," he says to the colonist, pointing to the holy book, "that I can read?"

The colonist says nothing.

"Gosh, that would really be a help."

The colonist says nothing.

"What is doing well?"

The colonist says nothing.

They come for him after lunch. He can hear the request go out over the loudspeaker: a number he recognizes as his own, the word *escort*, some initials he doesn't understand yet. Give him time.

He's told to move into the airlock. A soldier pulls a thin piece of rope to open the door to the cell and shuts it after he moves inside. So many different systems! He puts his hands through the hole and they cuff his hands and then open a hole at the bottom of the door and attach those cuffs to his shackled feet. They move swiftly, like a two-handed sailing team rigging for a quick turn.

Flanked and bound, he moves slowly down the hall. One of the soldiers—broad-shouldered, blond—seems almost cheerful today, freshly showered, a little bouncy, scented like a pansy. Inconsistent, he thinks, the kind of guy who should have been a stud but would rather socialize on the sidelines, winking at the crowd, leaping to his feet for fierce brief play on special teams only.

"Query," he asks. "They got rats here, soldier?"

Blondie stiffens and looks down at him, flinty. The prisoner is shorter since this whole thing started.

"I don't know about where you grew up?" he continues. "Where I grew up we had some good-sized rats, but I have a sense I ain't seen nothing yet." They're getting pissed off but something must be done. "Hey," he says quietly although he does not bow his head; no matter how hard it is to walk like this, shackled, you can keep upright if you go slow. "Forgive me if I'm out of line, here. I don't want to get anyone in trouble over the rodent situation."

"Old man, you could not get me in trouble in this world or another. You're just a piece of evidence."

"I suppose that's true," he says. He nods. "You're doing a hell of a job, soldier. All of you. I mean that."

They move down the corridor past two MPs with sidearms. "Spiders," says Blondie suddenly. If there's a rule against talking to prisoners, these guys don't seem to mind. "Ten-legged spiders. Big as your fist. Make your flesh rot and turn black."

"My goodness. What's the workaround?"

"Workaround is don't be a fucking bad guy." The young man loosens his grip on his shoulder. The strength of youth! How sore their muscles must be at the end of the day! A thin vein of pride pulses through him. He fights off a little smile. "Workaround is stay away from spiders," the soldier says.

Blondie knocks on a blue metal door and it opens into the same room he was in last night. There's the table. There's Jolman. There's the map again. There's a picture of him eating lunch with the petrochemical asshole. There's a picture of the asshole's assistant. There's their waiter. There's the asshole's driver.

"Let's start again," Jolman says.

After a few hours, Jolman leaves and a man who looks less ethnic but otherwise a lot like Jolman takes over. The new guy repeats all of the same questions, and he repeats all of the same answers. Then a few more hours and Jolman's back. Then the alter-Jolman. Then Jolman. When he starts to fall asleep, they wake him.

I'm going to have to speed this up, he thinks.

Afterward, he is chained together with the five other prisoners from his cell and taken outside. They kneel in the bright sun with their hands behind their heads. At first the air feels good but very soon it's only air. His arms begin to shake and burn and fall but he will not let them fall. He refuses to close his eyes and he refuses to let his arms fall. He is not sure if they are there for fifteen minutes or almost an hour. He watches the colonist but the colonist will not look at him. As they are brought back inside he speaks softly to the colonist. "I told them to punish me alone."

"No talking," a guard barks.

The colonist whispers something in the other language.

"I'll crack this thing," he whispers back. "I always do."

The interrogations are all the same but the ingredients are cooked up in different ways. Sometimes it is once a day, sometimes it is three times, sometimes a day goes by without any interrogations at all. Sometimes a whole day is an interrogation. The main operative is Jolman, but one day Mutt and Jeff are there! They look glum about their reassignment. And there are three others who appear occasionally, plus two high-ranking officers he sees once and then never again. There are visitors from the national agency and the central agency and the armies' agencies and a few he does not know where they are from. It seems possible they don't know either. He tells Jolman about his time wrestling and at college and in the service. He tells Mutt and Jeff about his father lying his way into a war. He tells one of the three others about moving around and growing up fast. He tells another one of them about his mother worrying when he went abroad. He tells the high-ranking officers about teaching rookie pilots to fly formations. He tells visitors from the national agency about his first election and his political life and the men he worked for and with, from his twenties through retirement. He tells visitors from the central agency about working for powerful men, some of the most powerful and opportunistic that ever lived, more cutthroat than he could ever be, which is why he could never climb that ultimate peg, although few men had ever served as long or as well as he. He tells the visitors from the armies' agencies about his brief turn as a lecturer, his longer stints as a businessman, a hired gun who fixed broken companies. He tells everyone about his travels. Time and time again they review dates, entry and exit dates, meetings with every person with whom he was tasked to talk. They review hundreds of pictures of people, over and over. They review every minutiae of the lunch with the petrochemical jerk, what they ate, who sat where, the minor players in attendance, but as much as he tells them, as much as he wracks his brain, he cannot see why or the connection. The guy was nobody, some friend of his buddy's buddy. They'd discussed some mineral rights but nothing ever came of it. He tells everyone the color of the tablecloth, the cars in the parking lot, each nuance of the conversation. They accuse him of nothing.

He knows where this is going. And they must know he knows it. It's the numbing before the knife. Yet if they think repetition and withholding will tamp his guard down, they'll be waiting a long time.

"You guys are worse than the press," he says. "You guys are worse than the treehuggers." But soon all humor is gone. "Please," he says, "either tell me what you're looking for or do whatever things they've cooked up for me. Which is it?"

No one will come close to answering except for Jolman. "We're not looking for one thing," Jolman says. "We are finding your intentions."

The colonist still won't talk to him. Then one morning he finds someone has placed a translated holy book on top of his other one. He opens them side by side. *All praise is due to God, the Lord of the worlds.* Pretty straightforward. He starts reading.

One afternoon they bring in someone important. Eight guards drag an enormous metal wardrobe into a solitary cell and bolt it into the wall. The prisoner has on three lines of chains around his ankles, waist, and wrists, all connected by a metal bar. They carry him in by the bar, a boar on a spit. A deeply foreign face, dark with the elements. This man has seldom been indoors. They rig him up inside the wardrobe and leave him. The man hangs there like an overcoat. Then he pulls himself up, trying to keep his weight off his wrists. After a minute the man lets go and dangles, making a strange noise halfway between an exhaled cry and inhaled moan.

A nasty business.

He listens to the stranger, watches him struggle and quit. I guess I'm not important, he thinks.

For interrogations, sometimes they chain him thoroughly and sometimes not. There is a big difference between interviewing a chained man and an unchained or semi-chained one. If only his arms were longer, it would be easy to get comfortable. But they're short, his arms. That may have won him a few arm-wrestling and push-up contests along the way, but it's not ideal for chains. Noted. Learned.

His cellmates are exercising. They jog around the edge of the wire, completing tiny laps every four to five seconds or so. They chant softly. The colonist leads the way. He used to be able to do one-armed push-ups to amuse and win over men like this. It doesn't matter. They are not allowed to do push-ups anyway. Strength is forbidden. The colonist still refuses to talk to him. He sits in the middle of the circling joggers, reading their holy book and watching for a while, and then he hops up and joins them. The men run faster. He runs faster. Do they think they can really get away from him? Around and around they go, these dangerous men chased down by the old man who used to sit in a big corner office, plotting their deaths. What would they do if they knew? He's never been in a schoolyard or a boardroom or any place that he couldn't win a place for himself. Starting over is not a problem for him. Not at all.

The men all stop running at once, but he does not stop. See?

There is a whiteboard in the hallway that he passes on his way to be interrogated. He finds his number up there in red. Red means normal. Green means sick. Yellow means something special. The wardrobe man is yellow. He dangles and doesn't sleep. Then there's blue. Blue means they send you to the island. Oh lord of the worlds, he thinks, please turn me blue soon.

He has no idea why Mutt and Jeff have followed him here, but their hatred for him is powerful stuff.

On one of his trips back from interrogation, he sees that his number on the big board has been changed to green. That night he begins to vomit dark and tarry. That's it, he thinks, they killed me. His gut curls him up. Prisoners are shouting. Get this sick jerk out of here. Hands hold him above the bucket of excrement. He tries to picture Mutt and Jeff standing in the bottom of the bucket, mouths propped open, their whole world raining with sick. But he is too far gone.

The guards call each other QB and Mistletoe and Psycho T. There's Frankenstein, Aruba, Skeletor. The blond soldier is QB. "Defense," QB tells him, "two years, college." One day QB gives him a book, some weird comic where an angel with her wings chopped off gets left behind, slumming in some seedy film noir town. "That's the real God," QB whispers. "You should check that out."

"But that's my God." Donald's feeling better, now. A virus, the doctor had said. He's feeling better enough now to want to find that doctor and laugh in his face. "Give me a break," he scolds QB. "We have the same God, you and me."

"What kind of fucked-up bad guy are you anyway?" says QB.

"You said it," he agrees. He moves QB three spots up the list.

Outdoors on the chain they cannot walk or move except in unison. That's once a week. Operation Sun-Bob. Everything is an operation. Every prisoner is Bob. Wash-Bob. Feed-Bob. Fun-Bob. He likes going outside but the process is so consumed with chains that somehow the colonist has it canceled.

"They listen to you?" he asks the colonist, but the colonist doesn't answer.

He is getting used to everything except sharing a bucket with six strangers for a toilet. Six strangers who won't talk to him, let alone joke about taking a crap. You can wrap yourself in a blanket but that's as good as it gets.

The rations come in ten different kinds, nothing cooked, nothing fresh.

Every six days is Wash-Bob. There's a caged washing area where they take his shackles off, give him one bucket of cold water. He's shocked that you can wash yourself with one bucket of cold water, but you sure can if you're careful. And perhaps if you're small. However, he seems to be the only one who's mastered this. His cellmates go for a wash and still come back smelling terrible.

A new wave of guards has arrived, young reservists from all over. Most of them are nicer but a few of them are more pissed off than ever. He has already seen one cycle of new guards arriving all gung ho and intelligent and then leaving defeated, cynical, depressed. It's a challenging system. He can see that. It is flawed. He'd tried to change things and made lots of enemies and nothing really changed. One of the new guards takes the holy books away from him. "You should be praying to me, asshole," the new guard says. "I'm the only God you have here."

He keeps his head down but the colonist is a troublemaker. The colonist leads the cell on a hunger strike to get more water. They get more water. The colonist complains vociferously until they are allowed to go outside again. The colonist stages a little play, a mocking tribute to the guards' system for moving prisoners in and out. The MPs look on suspiciously.

Everyone comes to the colonist for advice. They tell the colonist that they really did help the enemy just a little bit, or they were sold for bounty, or they were tortured into confessions abroad. He can understand these conversations now, a little bit, he's pretty sure. "I could be of use to you," he tells Jolman. "I'm learning their language." He rats them out, one by one: the wall-eyed man is guilty, the handsome one is not. "I'm not sure about the colonist. I'm really not. But I'll find out. Let me work on him. He's the key. I will find out. I think we're on to something." Jolman listens patiently. Of all of them, Jolman is the best listener.

The next day they take the colonist away. That night the special prisoner starts screaming. He's been shackled to the wardrobe thing for days, removed every four hours for questioning, and through it all has muttered madly to himself, but this screaming is in a new key. The guards don't like it. They try to quiet the special prisoner down, and when the special prisoner struggles they kick him in the back of the knee. There's a nerve there that incapacitates the leg. They unchain him and they scream at him and kick him in the nerve along the floor. It's a breakdown. Their training is falling apart.

"Stop!" Donald yells through the din and wire. "Please stop!" He's not sure anyone can hear him, and if they do they don't care. He would run and stop them if he could. That's not what people think about him, but he knows he would.

For three days there are no interrogations at all. The rumor is the special prisoner is dead. No one seems to know. Then a new wave of prisoners arrives. The colonist comes back, along with a man who has lost his legs in a minefield, in another war. This man half crawls around on stumps. Maybe this guy knows the one-legged horseman! This is what we're fighting against, people! he wants to tell someone. But who? Jolman seems to listen but he doesn't seem to hear.

"What about the colonist?" he asks Jolman. "Was I right? Did you get actionable intel?"

"Hard to say," says Jolman.

The waves of prisoners keep coming. It's a rotten process. One of the new guards catches his eye and they synch their eyebrows in disgust. "What a shithole," the guard says. "We should have you guys in the new facility before too long." "Won't that be nice," he says. The guard's a talker, he can see that. It's an opportunity. "You won't believe it," the guard says. "I bet. When?" He's survived. He can't evade. He won't resist. But maybe he can escape! Even if he fails, that might get someone's attention. Someone higher. As long as they don't kill him. Not like this. "It's not my job to know that." There's the phrase. He takes the hint and lets the guy stop talking. They both watch the new-Bobs file in until he sees someone he knows.

He gets as close to the wire as he dares and peers as the guards pass by with the new prisoner, and as they do, he meets Ed's eyes, or at least what used to be Ed's eyes but now look filled with dark smooth river stones resting in a shaved head tilting atop the jumpsuit. The basic infrastructure of Ed is there but everything else is gone.

He tries to find out more. "Finally got another white-Bob in here!" he congratulates the guard who took his holy books. Sometimes the ones who want to rub it in your face will actually tell you something by accident. "Where'd you find him?"

The guard chuckles. "You're a feisty little motherfucker, aren't you?"

Progress, he thinks.

One day he races the colonist. They are all exercising like usual but one by one the other men drop out until it is only him and the colonist. Everyone watches. The guards are laughing. The prisoners are smiling. The colonist keeps putting on these bursts of speed, but he catches up again and again. "Is that all you got?" he calls out, smiling. He turns around and backpedals. The guards cheer. One of the other prisoners tries to trip him but he sees it coming and hops over the outstretched foot, pirouetting in the air and landing right in stride. Amazing. Even the prisoners are laughing now. He's still amazing. The colonist shakes his head and stops, breathing hard, hands on knees.

His chest burns but he keeps running.

Later the colonist talks to him.

"I'm innocent," the colonist complains.

"Of what?"

"You sound like them," says the colonist.

"If we can give them someone, anyone, someone big," he whispers, "I can get us out of here."

"Maybe you're someone big." The man's breath stinks of soggy paper.

"Or maybe you."

The colonist shrugs and strolls away.

The next interrogation is different. He is taken from his cell and short-shackled, hands and feet closer together than usual, cuffs cinched extra tight. They force him to walk like this, bent over, the new guards batting him down if he tries to straighten up. He's invented himself a little dancing game to make walking like this more bearable. They have his body but he still has his mind, although he knows the point. The point is to make mind and body one.

The room is one he has not seen before. Mutt and Jeff stand in front him. Two new guys stand behind. Jolman is not there. Jolman doesn't seem to like Mutt and Jeff much either. Mutt's lost some weight.

"Who set up the lunch?" Jeff says.

"My office did. It's on my schedule. I was working for our government."

The sing-song could sing without him.

"You know what we're talking about."

"I'm getting tired of this shit," says Mutt. He realizes, with surprise, that they have not used profanity with him before.

"Don't you want to see your family again?" Jeff's pulling pictures from a folder: his wife, his children, his grandchildren, none of them photos he's ever seen. They have good photographers. Of course. We have everything. We or they? Most of the photos are first-rate, but there's a particularly nice one of Donald's son, black-and-white, with semi-professional lighting and deep-down laughing eyes. They are not as close as they could be, he and his son. He reaches over in his cuffs and picks up the photo. "Because it doesn't seem like you do," Jeff's saying. "You're being very selfish. Think of what could happen to them when they get sucked into this mess. When we bring them in."

Has Jeff been taking interrogation lessons? He imagines the man at home, rehearsing in front of a mirror or practicing on the kids. Repetition. Futility. Pride and ego. File and dossier. We know all.

"To see what they know."

"This is an excellent picture," Donald says.

"To jog your memory."

"How long do you think they'd last?"

The chair is pulled out from under him and he falls to the floor. Mutt's shoes are cheap and scuffed. "Get up," says one of the men behind him. "You've lost the right to sit."

"I've never minded standing."

"I've decided to send you somewhere," Jeff says. "Where you'll talk."

"A place with less," says Mutt.

"Under different."

"With fewer."

But this isn't standing. Short-shackled, a hunchback trying to meet their gaze. This is not standing at all.

"We just brought your pal back from there. He was playing the same games with us, but." Jeff snaps and wags two fingers at him, showing front and back. "Two hours it took. You might last three."

"Or one," says Mutt.

"He told us everything," Jeff says.

"And then some," Mutt says.

"Your ass is sunk."

"Blub blub blub."

"Go ahead," Donald says. "I'm not scared. Do it then, if you're going to do it. If that's what they want." He's scared but he's more angry. He can still get angry. That's a good sign. "You two make me sick."

One of the men behind him steps forward. "I'll take a minute with him," the man says, and the other men clear the room without a word. "Sit down," the man says, and he strides to the other side of the table. They sit in unison, a cozy church choir of two.

This man is tall. He is broad and middle-aged. He has an accent that is hard to pin down. His mouth was originally shaped by another language. He has spent time in the field, unlike Mutt and Jeff. He's shot people and been shot at. He does not bruise or bleed easily. "I guess you're pretty familiar with all this," the man says. "I guess it doesn't surprise you."

"We've been around, haven't we."

"That's the job," the man says.

"Yes it is." He wants to lean back but the chains won't let him. He has to keep his weight forward like some eager schoolboy. "I'm obviously very interested in what you have to say." Somewhere between his liver and his kidney he's stashed something in anticipation of this moment. It's still sharp. Shiny.

"There are some people who are very happy to see you in here, of course. But not everyone."

He waits. Sometimes things are going better than they appear from the inside.

"There are. Differences of opinion. About the path forward."

"How do you see things?" The man has done this hundreds of times, maybe thousands. But so have I, he thinks. "Let's start from there."

"I think," the man says, "I think we all make mistakes. I think we all listen to people we shouldn't listen to. I think we trust people we shouldn't trust. I think some people sow and never reap. Would you agree with that?"

"Of course I would." He has heard the man's voice before.

"Of course you would. And let's agree that you're never getting out of here unless you adjust."

"Okay. I don't know that to be true but we'll agree." He doesn't want this conversation to end.

"It's true."

"Good. We live in this world. Not the one that could be. We understand that."

"Right now you're the goat. Time to bring in the shepherds. Not the dogs. Not the herd."

"That's always been the goal," he says, still trying to place the man's voice.

"Well here we are," the man says.

This man was at the house. The third man in the kitchen. This is his chance. This is what he has been holding out for, why he has refused to make stuff up to satisfy their swift desire. There is no long term without a short term. "Okay," he says.

The man frowns. The man has frowned a lot. The lines are deep and worn. People probably make fun of this man, too. But not here.

The man places a plain manila envelope on the table. It's an envelope that could have ended up anywhere—in a middle-manager's drawer, holding odd receipts—but has flown halfway around the world to a little room where history is being made. The man pulls a new set of pictures from the envelope. "We're filling in the case."

"Yes." *Case.* A great word.

"Corroborated. Annotated."

"Yes."

"But we're not releasing it."

"No."

The man is spreading the pictures across the table, flipped for the prisoner to see. Faces stare up at him. He doesn't have his glasses but he knows them. He has been shown hundreds of pictures but this is the first time these faces have been on display. He could never not know them! "A case like this is complex," the man is saying. "But it's compelling because it reaches in every direction. It goes down," the man says, tapping his finger on the photo pyramid of his lawyers, his assistant, his secretary. His military subordinates are notably missing. "It goes sideways." And there're his rivals, the men and women he finally lost out to, through no fault of his own. There's his connected friend from college. "But what we are interested in is up." The man taps the two pictures at the top. There's Donald's boss on the right. But it's the big face on the left that smiles out at him, the nice skin, the closed-mouth smile hiding crooked teeth, the thin upper lip, the wide familiar forehead of his once protégée, sometimes colleague, and always friend. "Yes," the third man says. "The cancer starts somewhere and then metastasizes. You can knock it down, but it will come back. You're right there in the middle of it, directing traffic. Everyone scrambles around to figure out where it started, how it moves around, but that's not what we want. We want the thing itself."

He focuses on the picture of his friend. Not that he's even thinking about it, but he needs time. And then suddenly he is thinking about it. His friend betrayed him once, the year he threw his hat into the big ring. Only time could fix it, but time did. Ha! And they think he no longer knows apples from oranges?

He won't betray anyone. He'll rot here and die. The pictures of his friends and colleagues give him purpose and strength. And yet. His head is still bent to their faces but he flicks his eyes up at the man and what does he see? Uncertainty. A thin patina, but uncertainty nonetheless. The third man may be rogue. There really are factions. Someone wants to fry him. Someone wants to fry his friend. Someone wants to step on his back to get ahead. And someone, somewhere, wants to let him go. They all want to use him. This is the first offer. It's a bad one. It's not even a real offer. But you have to have an offer to get another one. The man is watching him. It's all right. He should be thinking about this. Anything else would be more suspect.

"I'm not sure I understand," he tells the third man. He meets the man's stare. He has to betray someone. That's what the stare tells him. And, all bluster aside, he has a list for that, too. "You're missing a few," he says, nodding at the pictures in front of him.

"Who?" says the third man.

"Who wrote the rules?" he says.

"You did," says the third man.

"I wrote rules." Climb, conserve, confess. "And based on the assumptions, those rules were right. But the assumptions weren't mine, and they weren't his or his or his. I know who made them, I know how you can find them. I will help you with that."

The third man examines his forehead, as if there's a display screen up there scrolling data instead of five lifetimes' worth of wrinkles, five or maybe more. "I've heard you're a tough bastard."

"I'm old. I'm locked up. I'm not looking too tough these days, am I?"

"Yeah," the third man says. "You don't seem too tough. Still." Then the third man scoops up the pictures like playing cards and pops them back in the folder, like a job interview coming to a swift and decisive close. "You *will* help us."

"I will. I am."

"You're really not." The third man stands. "You're really not even close."

"Am I conflicted? Of course. But I also understand the situation. I understand it as well as anyone."

"I don't believe you. No one does. But that's not even the point." The man shakes his head. "This is simply about behavior, you know. Those couple of dogs that Pavlov couldn't get to work the way they were supposed to—he had to castrate them and starve them for three weeks. Eventually they worked just like the other ones. But it took extra work, and it took time." The third man knocks on the door.

Progress, in a sense.

They cuff his hands and feet together and put him in a cell by himself, away from the other prisoners. There's a thin carpet on the concrete floor and a little shawl. He waits for a while for someone to come back, and then sits against the wall, but when he starts to fall asleep a guard appears and wakes him up. Then the music starts. It's so loud he can't tell what it is at first. Then he recognizes it, not the song per se but the modern urban drone of it. They must assume this is music he would not like. And they are right. Still, somehow he falls asleep again. The guard appears and wakes him up.

He's not sure how much time has passed, is passing. He tries to structure his thoughts. Regimens lend structure to the void. The first cycle is scenarios: agree to everything, agree to most things, make something up, hold out, resist. If they would only bring him back to the other prisoners maybe he could get some useful information. The second cycle is home: his ranch, and the house, and back in one of his childhood homes, the narrow place they lived in, the apple tree outside, and then he closes his eyes but the guard comes in and pokes him until he stands up again. The third cycle is the arc of history, and the fate of the old enemy that built these walls that house him now, and what happened to that enemy here, in these mountains, the beginning of their end, brought down by the one-legged horseman, and how history's arc will bury this enemy too, although who knows about the next one. History suggests that we might be luckier to be vanquished from without than left to our own decline. It's the choice between being shot high off the rampart or hanging from the shower curtain. Then the guard is poking him awake with a long baton. The music gets louder. He falls asleep again. The baton again. Three guards come in with a stepladder and fasten a chain to a metal bar along the ceiling and fasten his handcuffs to the chain. They leave him there to dangle. He is an important person.

They've given him some slack, but he has to keep his arms up. If he falls asleep the cuffs bite into his wrists and wake him up. The pain of holding your arms up is intense, like a meat needle jammed in deep behind each shoulder blade. The choice is between pain here or there. He sets small goals and achieves them. But the cycles are shrinking. A cycle with his arms up thinking about all of the great generals who were not tactical geniuses but out-trained everyone, then a cycle dangling there wondering about his buddy, then an arms-raised cycle for his horse, a dangling cycle for his grass, an arms-up cycle for wrestling, and he keeps that up until the woman next door starts screaming.

When she stops screaming they come and take him down. Then they leave and she starts screaming again. He calls for the guards but they do not come. Meals are slid beneath the door. Every time he falls asleep the woman next door starts screaming. It's not a strong scream. She's not young. But she screams and screams.

He wakes up sitting across a table from Jolman. How long has he been there? His first thought is of the woman, but he doesn't say anything. Jolman watches him. Back in his city office hangs a satellite photo of the world's most isolated nation at night, a patch of pitch darkness amid civilization's lights. He's always been drawn to this photo for the reprehensibility it represents, but only now, after two days alone, or three days, he doesn't even know, does he understand why. There is nothing worse, is there?

Jolman tosses a passport on the table. "Some of the dates don't match up," he says.

"Okay." The sight of an object from the outside world sends a jolt of euphoria through him. He wants to touch it.

"They sent us some things of yours." Jolman opens the passport and they both stare at the picture of his wife. He reaches. He can't help it. Jolman pulls the passport away. "Oh," says Jolman, "this one's yours," swapping it for another.

They're bluffing. She can't be here. These are just the means. They're going to open this passport to a photo of the severed head of his horse. He's not a peasant. He knows what they're doing!

"We'll go through it again," he tells Jolman. "I am cooperating. I understand how serious you are. I will do anything you want."

Jolman leans in suddenly. His shoulders are bigger than they seem. He pictures the soldier at the base gym, grunting under a loaded bar. "I've decided to send you to the island," he says in quiet voice.

"Okay." He tries not to let his relief show. "I just want you to know that I'm trying."

"I know," says Jolman. "I know you are. But it's been decided. It's for the best. I think it could be the beginning of the end for you."

He nods. "I know how hard it is to believe the word of someone you don't trust. And I know your orders are not to believe or trust me."

"What I believe is not important," says Jolman. "I have filed my reports." Is that a wrinkle around Jolman's immigrant eyes? This job will take its toll.

"Good," says Donald. "That's all you can do." He feels stronger in a room with Jolman, stronger than he has felt for days.

"I shouldn't tell you this, but I will," says Jolman. "The issue at this point is not your cooperation. The issue is that you are still capable of not cooperating. That is what must change."

They shave his head again and put him back with the others. On the way back to their cell he sees that his number is indeed now blue. Ed is nowhere to be seen.

"I'm leaving," he tells the colonist, who has returned to the group during his absence.

"I testified against you," the colonist says.

"I understand."

"I signed a confession."

"It doesn't matter."

"No, it doesn't. I'm going to die here."

Donald bows his head slightly to the colonist and murmurs the words in the enemy's tongue. He doesn't know exactly what he's saying but the meaning is clear: God's will be done. An affirmation of meaning that crosses every faith, and why not?

When they come to take him from his cell, he's ready. But the guards merely remove him from the cage and walk him fifteen feet to the next cage down. It's empty. They shove him through the airlock. He gazes around at the identicalness of it all. Except that now he's alone again. Why would they lie about the island? Why would they do this? He's been stupid. He knows he must plan ahead knowing that every plan may be a lie and every plan may change. Small goals, he thinks. They add up.

And then everyone starts laughing: the guards, the colonists, the prisoners across the way, where he sees Ed again, finally, smiling with the rest. A prank! Everyone is looking at the colonist. He clearly has arranged the whole thing. How? They leave him there for a few minutes while they laugh and laugh.

He smiles a tight smile and then gives them teeth, applauding them. He spins in a slow circle, clapping, and then he starts to bow. He bows to the guards. He bows to Ed. He bows to the colonist and his old cellmates. He bows to the hundreds and then they take him away again. They put an orange jacket on him and an orange hat and tell him to use the bathroom. The guards look different. They're wearing jungle fatigues instead of desert khakis. They put black spray-painted goggles on him, giant earmuffs, facemask, chains running across his chest and legs. A guard tells him his new number and he feels someone writing on his back. In the cargo-hold someone pops a pill in his mouth. He doesn't even think about it. The pill rushes across his tongue on a spray of water from a plastic bottle. He closes his mouth and when he wakes up he can smell the ocean.

7

Small brown sunbaked rocks scroll by beneath his feet. There's heat. There's humidity. His shackles have been changed. His hands are cuffed and there's a chain going from his waist to his ankles. Then he is inside again, taken in and out of shackles. A doctor looks him over and takes an x-ray of his chest. A shower, an orange jumpsuit. They remove his surgical mask and give him a peanut butter sandwich. He knows the manufacturer. He remembers when they got the contract. Soup to nuts. Built half of these prisons, too.

His cell is slightly larger than a bed except there is no bed. There's a metal shelf and a squat-style toilet. The walls are that green metal honeycomb they use in basements to seal off dangerous machinery from the public. There's a blanket and a thin camping mat. The blanket's made of plastic so it can't be torn or ripped. Suicide proof. He knows who makes those as well.

Still, he is glad he's on the island. The island is closer to civilization. To family. To her. Not that it matters. But it does matter.

The morning is busy. First the call to prayer coming over the loudspeakers, then prisoners in prayer, and then, a while later, the national anthem.

"Honor bound!" a soldier calls out.

"To defend freedom," comes the answer.

A little later a guard brings him a cooked meal of rice, green peas, and a boiled egg all mixed together. There's tea and powdered milk in Styrofoam cups, both cold. He drinks the milk but that's all. They haven't given him any toilet paper and he doesn't feel like asking.

It's a tight ship here. Every few minutes it seems like a soldier peeks into his cell. He can hear other prisoners but he can't see anyone. There's no one in the cells next to his.

On the second day he is taken out of his cage in the middle of the night. There's a table set up. Jolman sits waiting.

"This is a surprise," he tells Jolman. But is it? Should he know that this is how things work? He can't remember anymore. His father lost his mind the old-fashioned way. Maybe that's what's going on here.

Jolman doesn't say anything. He shuffles through his papers as if there's one with answers on it.

"I have a new idea, Jolman."

Jolman looks up but then the door opens and in walk Mutt and Jeff and a man he hasn't seen before. Mutt opens a folder and places six typed pages in front of him on the table.

"We want you to read and sign this," Mutt says.

"What's this, Jolman?" But Jolman has his own copy, it seems, and is reading it, too. Donald leans forward and skims the papers quickly. He is sleepier than usual, and more relaxed. "You've written my confession for me."

"You have to," Jolman says. His voice sounds different here, lower and more menacing. Either this is the real Jolman or he's putting on a show. "Otherwise you'll be here forever before anyone even looks at your case."

"Then a summary tribunal," says Mutt.

"A formality before conviction," adds the stranger.

"It's going to be one short trial!" says Mutt.

"They'll take the evidence at face value," says Jeff.

"And then they'll execute you," Mutt explains. "You'll wait and wait and then suddenly."

He knows that isn't true. But he also knows there are three categories of interrogation used here and this is only one of them. He leans over the pages again. It doesn't even sound like him. The confession is ridiculous. No one would ever believe it. It's a document written by a simpleton. Flabby and repetitive, barely proofread, too long by half. It's full of lies, exaggerations, and presumptions. There are names in there he's never heard of. In it he confesses to funneling money to the enemy, meeting with senior enemy members and contributing to their success. But even the basic facts of the document are wrong. In the same sentences it mentions a meeting between him and a dictator twenty years ago and an unrelated plan to build an enemy camp last year. He wants to correct them. Is it really possible that his country's being run by idiots who don't even know that not all enemies are the same, that the dictator's people and the people building the enemy camp have spent five hundred years trying to wipe each other off the map? Or is that just to piss him off, too? It doesn't matter; it's false. Or most of it is. All the travel dates are correct, including a few less known trips that they somehow know about. He sure didn't tell them. The lunch with the petrochemical asshole is not even mentioned.

Yes, yes, he thinks. They have data and numbers, but their interpretations and sums are wrong. Is this a misstep? He pictures brows wrinkling on the mainland. A worried hippie shreds some documents, a jilted general dodges questions. They know they can only keep him here so long, so close, before the system spits him out. This confession is a Hail Mary, and he's going to intercept it in the endzone.

"Have you read this?" he asks Jolman.

"You should have seen the draft before," says Jolman. "You'd have thought we were cuckoo."

"There's no way I'm signing this."

"You could be shot by a firing squad, do you understand?" Jeff says.

"On video," says Mutt.

"They've built an execution chamber here. I've seen it."

"Have you forgotten about your wife? Your family?"

"You don't have a choice," Jolman says bluntly.

It's freezing. Will the air conditioner always be up this high? Forever? You need an offer to get another offer. No one—no judge, no general, no faction—will ever believe this. It's his chance. He grabs the document and signs.

They give him a beige jumpsuit and a roll of toilet paper and move him to a different cell block. The early morning prayers wake him. Men's voices rise in every direction. He is outside now. He can smell the sea again. In the darkness he stays curled beneath his plastic blanket, listening to them. He doesn't understand everything. Prayer is better than sleep, they chant, as he drifts away again.

Later that morning a guard comes and opens his cage and hands him his glasses. The world's edges leap out at him. And there's a softness in the guard's face, a pleasure there in helping a fellow man.

"Thank you," he says. He imagines his glasses loaded on planes in padded pouches, tagged and catalogued. The premeditation of it!

"Sure," the guard says. "You earned 'em." The man is large and pale and older, much older than the others. "Get your whites in no time."

"Right," he says. He's seen prisoners in white. He knows it's better although he can't remember why. Did he once read that orange was the color of insanity?

"This place," the guard says, waving his hand in a theatrical rainbow, "is not like where you were. It's all cause and effect. Merit system." A hollow sound of hammering cuts down from above, and the guard glances murderously skyward. "We're trying to kill those little motherfuckers," the guard says. The sound comes back, louder this time. Woodpeckers.

"They don't go easy, do they?" he says.

"Protected, too." The guard grins and jags his eyebrows. There's a story behind an old soldier like this one. An important story, useful. The guard shuffles back from the cage door, glances at his notes. "You're up for some exercise this afternoon."

"Get a sonic system," he tells the guard. "For the birds."

"Oh, man." The guard laughs. "Love to see my CO's face if we put in for that."

"There's a procurement code in the system already. Bundle it into the beans and bullets. See what happens." It's the kind of thing that drove him crazy at the top, looking down, trying to plug the endless leaks, but could he be any less at the top now?

The guard laughs again. "Got all kinds in here, don't we." The pale guard rubs his lips. "Well I'll let you know how that works out."

"I'll be here."

The old guard's name is Grady. A veteran of another era, another war, also complicated. "Hell, I think those same rules should apply," Grady says. "Prisoners are prisoners. I don't agree with half this stuff at all."

"There are bad people in this world," he tells Grady. "There's evil and mischief."

"Yeah," Grady says. "But all of you? I don't see it. Either you should be sent home or you should be treated like POWs. I know y'*all* can't be guilty."

"Most, though. Trainers, bomb guys, bombers, bodyguards, financiers, recruiters, facilitators, researchers, video makers, writers, cooks, babysitters, farmers. United in their commitment to fight off free societies and cause the deaths of innocent men, women, and children."

"Apples and oranges," Grady says. "But there must be innocent people, too. There always are."

"Well that's true." He leans as close as he can to the wire without touching. "That's always true. The world of intel is imperfect. How many guilty people are you willing to let free? How many innocent people are you willing to lock up?"

"Guy's in a house taking shots at me. Women and children in there, civilians. Take out the house?"

"Sometimes."

"Sometimes is right." Grady wipes his face down with one big hand.

"I don't expect you to believe me. In fact you shouldn't. You don't have the right information. But someone does. Someone up the chain."

"Maybe. Or maybe you're lying. That's the nutshell, isn't it. Who knows what and if they're lying."

"There must be a reason I ended up in here, right? You have to assume that. Then again, some of these guys in here were sold for cash. And look at me."

"I don't know. I don't know about you."

"Information," Donald says. He doesn't want to rush this. You plant a seed. "This isn't an army of soldiers you're facing. It's a confederacy of spies that's trained to lie before, during, and after imprisonment. You wouldn't still be in the service if your job was to tell a man you were his friend and then shoot him in the back."

"No I wouldn't."

"And yet that's what's happening to me. What did they tell you? That I'm a traitor? Or a spy?"

Grady doesn't say anything for a while. "Hell," the guard says finally "all I know is that I shouldn't still be in anyway. Cost me just about everything except my truck."

"Nice truck though, right?"

"Goddamn right."

He hears about the truck for a while and then Grady starts to move off down the line.

"You could do one thing," he calls after the guard. "Paper. A pencil. I'm trying to jot things down."

Grady doesn't answer but waves amicably back over his shoulder.

There are prisoners in the cage beside his but they won't speak to him. He tries. But they won't.

The guards shoot a woodpecker the next day. The young one who grew up on the tobacco farm comes to show him. It has a red breast and some red around its chin and the top of its head is missing. It's so small.

"They'll be back," he tells the guard. "There's more where that came from."

"That's what she said," the young guard says. He must be nineteen, maybe twenty. The other guards call him Smoke. "I'll kill 'em all."

"We always did treat their spies differently," says Grady. "In the war." He slides a short stack of paper into Donald's cell and rolls a two-inch pencil in after it.

The weather is getting hotter. He's asked for more water but they keep forgetting and Grady isn't around.

He has not seen Mutt or Jeff or Jolman or anyone he knows since the night of his confession. He can't tell if his gambit is paying off or is costing him. There is a new interrogator. A youngish woman named D or maybe Dee, with long mousy blond hair. They're in a little hut in the middle of a big gravel compound, where one half is a cell and the other is a meeting area. Every day he's taken out to the cell to wait for Dee, and then they move him next door and chain him to the eyebolt in the floor and shackle his arms. Dee sends the guards away. He hasn't been alone in a room with anyone since the third man.

"How are you holding up?"

"Just fine, thank you. You've got some good soldiers working here. Good bones in place."

"Oh?" She seems amused.

"There's room for improvement. I could use some plastic shoes instead of flip-flops, something to read. I keep asking for more water." Metallic sounds click through from the camp outside. Someone is always working on something. It's a busy place.

"Maybe I can help."

"You've read my confession?"

"Yes."

"Convincing, huh?"

"And you've been writing something else?"

"Letters to my wife."

"Of course."

"Are you married, Dee?"

She is. She tells him about her husband, a contractor. She tells him about the small city they live in. They've changed tactics, he thinks. They've sent the angel. Is she in charge of making sure the confession goes down easy? That he pleads guilty when the time comes?

"You'll be tried by a military commission," Dee says. "Once the lawyer is appointed, we won't be able to meet without his or her explicit agreement."

"I understand," he says. "It's a fair system. Just let it work."

"You're not what I expected," Dee says. She passes him a magazine stamped APPROVED.

"I think we're getting along just fine."

The five men next door have started talking to him. He knows a few words of their language, and two of them speak a bunch of his. The weird thing is that these two are the ones he isn't sure about. Of the remaining three, he's certain that two are real bad guys and the third is probably innocent. The bad guys smell like bombs. The innocent guy smells like grass and looks too scared and clueless to be guilty of anything. But the two who speak his language, he really doesn't know.

One morning he wakes up with the image of a painting in his head. It's the one from his dining room of the inside of a boat, with the wooden ribs evoking the belly of the whale, which was why he liked it. His wife and he did not see eye to eye on art. She sought beauty but he wanted a story. He understood that art didn't have to tell stories, but why the hell not? This one did. The ship was a whale. The viewer was stuck in its belly to contemplate his sins. What have I done, oh lord? Now there's a story.

He tells one of the guys next door—a prisoner who for unclear reasons has been allowed to keep his beard—about his dream. "God sent this man to prophesy destruction," Donald explains, "but he chickened out. Then he ends up in the belly of the whale for three days and nights."

"We have that story, too," the bearded man says. A connection! Their conversations seldom get far. "He tried to teach the stupid people but gets difficulty. He runs away and the big fish eats him. The fish vomits and his skin falls off. A plant gives him new skin and he converts a hundred thousand men." He mentions the name of two towns, one where the man was buried, the other where the stupid people lived.

"Both in the war zone," Donald says.

"Yes."

"I would like to hear more of your stories," he tells the bearded man.

"Another time," replies the bearded man.

The guards talk freely with him these days but little else happens. They don't give him a white jumpsuit. They don't give him a lawyer. Every day he sits down with Dee for a while to go over the details of his confession once again, which is repetitive, because he refuses to embellish the lies they've already scripted for him. He sticks to their story. She doesn't seem to have another offer. He wants to get in front of a court or a tribunal or someone charged with judgment, not analysis. Analysis will only get you so far. At some point, judgment must kick in. He imagines a committee of men that look like his father, his friend, his boss, his associates, the men he used to work with day after day sitting behind a table with stern looks on their pouchy faces. Innocent. Guilty. What they do with the uncertain ones—that will be their test! Lock them up, he thinks. The price of ruining one innocent life is steep but it is less than the price of thousands of lives destroyed by lenient misjudgment. Millions. If this were business you could risk a loss, a bad investment, a bad assessment that did some damage to your profits and your company. But this is not business, and the damage, when it comes, is to your country and your people, and no matter how small it might be—two people, ten people, thirty, several hundred—the loss is unacceptable. And yet for the accused and their families, their loss of having innocent fathers and brothers and uncles locked up, two, ten, thirty, several hundred, that loss is unacceptable. Well that's what war is, isn't it, a dispute over who will accept the unacceptable? Only weakness believes you can do right without wrong. Strength knows they're indivisible.

"If you all weren't actually bad guys before," Grady is saying, "you will be now." He's back from wherever he went to. Another post, a leave, a sickness, he doesn't say.

"But I'm not," he tells Grady. "I never was and I never will be. Can't you see that by now?"

Grady looks him up and down.

"Would I really be here if I was a spy?" Donald says. "Think about it. Spies usually get shot."

"Take no prisoners," says Smoke. "Keep it simple stupid, and send my ass back home."

"I've seen that," says Grady, shaking his head. "You don't want that, kiddo, believe me. It's not that simple. Go down that road and you'll never really go home again."

"When you think about what these people are willing to do?" Donald says. "I think we treat them well, considering."

"What's this we, white man?" Smoke says.

"Ha!" Donald says. He points a finger at Smoke and grins with real pleasure.

Smoke looks at Grady and circles a finger around his ear.

The next day Smoke's upset. His girlfriend dumped him. Grady looks amused.

"My leave's in two weeks," Smoke says. "I'm not coming back to this shithole."

"We'll miss you too, cupcake," Grady says.

"One day this place will be in a museum," says Smoke. He doesn't elaborate.

The evening anthem begins to play, and both soldiers salute an invisible flag. Then, halfway through, the sounds of prayer rise up around them. The anthem cranks up louder. The prayers get louder, too. Then the soldiers start singing at the top of their lungs. He realizes he's singing, too. The guards start laughing.

"Nothing of what you hear and half of what you see," says Grady.

"What's it gonna take, old man?" says Smoke.

He sleeps on the camping mat under his suicide blanket. That night he has a dream. In the dream his youngest daughter has been kidnapped and the man who knows where she is sits in front of him, bound to a chair, refusing to talk.

"You will," Donald says. He's in his kitchen. Everything is familiar. There are newspapers on the breakfront, one after another, laid out with the headlines visible but unreadable. The blender is filled with something colorful and pulpy. He reaches for a carving knife from the woodblock near the refrigerator. "Would you like another chance? There aren't any more."

He leans forward and slides the knife below the man's kneecap. He wants to know, where is his girl? What's happened to her? She was such a good child. She went to his same college and then moved west, became a doctor, a psychiatrist of all things. The man screams, ejaculates a spray of blood across his terrycloth robe.

The man before him is screaming but Donald can't hear his screams. The silence is noticeable. It's unfamiliar. There's no hum from the electricity, no movement in the air. Watching the man scream is like watching a television set with no sound, and then it's like he's underwater, or the ground has left him, and then he is there, in his kitchen, and the noise bursts through like a fire alarm. He withdraws the knife, jabs it into the man's thigh.

"Where?"

"I don't know!" the man cries. "I don't know what you're asking!"

"My girl," he says. He turns to the shelf to grab her picture. There's a picture there of his wife and son sitting at the end of a dock. But the girl in the picture is not his daughter. She's different, younger, darker. She doesn't look anything like his daughter, who's always been blond with skin as white as a bar of soap. He looks again to the man, bound and bloody, seated in his kitchen. The resemblance is obvious. It's this man's daughter in the picture. The same nose, the same hair. How do you know what you know?

"It doesn't hurt," the bound man says. "Not at all."

8

There's always a table. Dee sits on the other side. There's always a table and always Dee, but something is different today. Her hair? She's cut it? Dee is not pretty but not plain either. She could be his second cousin's daughter. That's what she looks like, Dee.

"Do you know this man?" The man in the photo has a long white beard, a black turban piled over his head, a robe with a sash tied around the waist. He carries a stick in one hand and he's walking in what looks like mountains. The air looks thin, the colors sucked out of everything but his face. The thought that he could know this man!

"No," he says. "Who is he?"

For a moment he thinks she's going to say something funny: *That's the guy who's screwing your wife!* But that's not funny. The fact is, he has been thinking about his wife lately. In a sexual way. A way that he hasn't thought about his wife in a long time.

"I can't tell you that," she says. He knows of course. No current information. Not that he even knows what current means anymore.

"Dee," he says. "Have you read the letters I've written to my wife?"

"They've been read," she says.

"Does she get them? Can you tell me anything about her?" He asks about the lawyer, sometimes, but the answer is always the same. They pretend this is how the system works, but he knows it isn't.

"I know. We're working on it." She flicks a stray bang from her eye with a cream-polished index finger. "Can you tell me anything else about attacks being planned against our cities?"

"Do you know how long I've been here?" he says. He would like her to answer, because he's not sure he knows, but she waits him out. "If I did know anything at one point, what would I know now? Where would the information come from?"

Dee shrugs her shoulders. She's not that interested. She's just doing her job. She's the good cop. She has him unshackled, except for the handcuffs. Of course, there's a guard at the door. But couldn't he maybe? Couldn't he lunge across the table, get his shackles around her throat, grab her tongue with his teeth and bite it off and spit it at the guard rushing forward? Where do these thoughts come from? The image reminds him of the dream he had. The blood and the violence. And then this morning, the thoughts of sex and his wife. It's these places opening up in his mind, rooms he's never been in. Anyway, it's a thought, not an action. The table is wide, it would be almost impossible to get across.

She stares at him. A soldier with a clean face and short mousy blond hair. Who does she really remind him of? So many soldiers in his career. He has the urge to tell her about his own military service again. The difference between the Navy and the Air Force, with its little rules for everything, while Navy pilots know rules change when everything is fluid. The world is mostly water. That's why soldiers prefer air support from the Navy over the Air Force. The Navy gets shit done.

Why is she looking at him like that? Where does this come from? Urges and thoughts he can't understand.

"There was a woman in the other place," he says suddenly. "A prisoner."

"Yes?"

"I never saw her but I heard her."

"Who was she?"

"I don't know. She was screaming."

"Who do you think she was?"

"I don't know!"

Two kicks at the door. Dee stands up and backs away from him. Has he crossed some line without realizing it? The door cracks open and she's gone.

He's been working on his confession. Dee's given him a copy and he's rewriting it. Annotating it, really. He only has a two-inch pencil so the notes are shorthand. He puts a check mark next to things that are correct and an asterisk for things that require correction and a minus sign with a circle around it for places where things are wrong or missing. Sometimes the minus sign/circle combo is so small it looks more like a face. Not a smiley face or a frowny face. A dead face. There are lots of things missing. He resists the urge to rewrite for voice or syntax or style. He wants his argument to be short and mathematical.

The next day they bring him off to interrogation after lunch. Except instead of the usual place they load him into a truck and take him to the other end of the camp. The room they bring him to is very small and deep down in the ground. Dee isn't there. No one is. He sits at the table and waits. No one comes for what seems like a long time. It might be an hour. He's not sure. He can hear voices outside. They're close and then they're far away and then they're close again. Finally the door opens again and in walks the third man, an officer, and the kid he saw at the library, weeks or months or years ago.

The kid looks older. He's wearing a dark suit that doesn't look right on him. The kid slides to the corner of the room farthest from him and leans against the wall. It occurs to him that what he has been doing in these interrogations is not unlike writing his autobiography or a memoir. Is that what this is about?

"How's that book coming?" he asks the kid. But the kid doesn't look at him. This kid! The hippies have come to check on him at last! The third man walks around the table. He's holding a roll of paper in his hand like a declaration. He unfurls the roll and there's the confession again.

"You were involved in planning the attacks," says the third man.

"That's false," he says. "That's just false. I was told to sign it. I was cooperating."

"So you lied."

"No."

"Stop wasting time with this pig," says the officer.

The third man glares at the officer. Is it a code? "You shut up," the third man tells the officer.

"I was told to sign it," he says again. "I was cooperating. If you looked down from Mars you— "

The third man places a hand on his shoulder and then slaps him across the cheek. "Get up."

He gets up. The third man slaps him in the stomach. The third man slaps him on the shoulder. He's not bleeding but he can feel his blood wilding through him. He's so awake. He's so clear. The third man grabs his collar and rips downward, tearing his jumpsuit down to his ankles. The third man rips his boxer shorts off him, almost causing him to fall, but the officer or kid must be holding him steady, too. The third man grabs him by the hair and slams his chest against the wall. The third man presses his forehead against the wall and pushes his feet back on either side until his weight is on his brow.

"Stay there," the third man says.

9

He's in another camp the guards won't say the name of. He's wearing orange again. Burlap is what it feels like. At first he does push-ups and sit-ups in his cell. He once won bets this way, but not like this. This bet is about what it's like to be an animal. Six feet by eight feet, the size of a large mattress. Except he doesn't have a mattress. He has a thin foam camping pad. His body aches from sleeping on hard surfaces. Bright lights shine on him. The walls are solid now, the way they are in a maximum-security prison, and there's no natural light. The windows are more like narrow slits than windows, and they can't be seen through anyway. The lights never turn off. No one talks to him. A guard sits outside his cell writing down the number of push-ups he does, the sit-ups. He still has some paper and the little two-inch pencil, so he writes. Notes for his book. He hired his buddy at the do-good agency. The job was to kill it. But they stripped it down and made it work. People were pissed. But they realized these two could make anything work. Even government.

Soon the writing becomes scattered. He can hear other prisoners praying in the morning, but he never sees them. He is alone.

Twice a week he's taken out for recreation. The three-piece suit is put on—

handcuffs, ankles, waist, connected—and he's walked to an outdoor yard. The yard is just a bunch of fence covered in thick green fabric. It's as large as a normal bedroom and not nearly as large as the bedroom he shared with his wife. He can't see through the fence but he can see the sky. That's the difference. He walks in circles for fifteen minutes, then a shower, then back to the cage.

The only other time he leaves his cell is for interrogations. At first there are none. Day after day he waits for the third man to come, but no one comes. Then they begin again. They wake him and bring him to the room. They take photographs, finger- and footprints, blood, hair follicles, biometric eye scans. Three men he's never seen before question him for hours, rotating one at a time. Can this still be part of a strategy? He doesn't even know what he's saying anymore. He used to be so careful with his words. His mother taught him that. He was famous for it. His words. Now he's losing them, one by one. He hands a word over and it's gone forever. He falls asleep in mid-sentence and they shake him awake or lean him against the wall again. What was it he said? There was a complaint about people being forced to stand. "Why only four hours?" he wrote. "I stand eight to ten hours a day." That was famous, too. He was a big man then. Fearsome. Tiger Teams. Copper Green. Make sure this happens. Make sure that. How did they define torture? Organ failure. But the mind is not an organ. The mind is ours to do with what we can, for good or bad. They've been told his mind is bad and so the goal is to make it fail. Will isolation do that? Will stress positions? Will strapping him to a table and fake-drowning him? You can't fake-drown character, he thinks. Maybe that's what it will take for them to know.

One day he kneels on his mat, pressing his forehead into the floor. He's not praying. Or he doesn't mean to be. He's pressing his head into the floor. He's trying to think straight. He lifts his head slightly, then bumps it against the floor, a couple more times. He knows the guard is writing everything down. He should be careful. If he split his head open, what would come out? After the third time he stops. He's still, kneeling. Waiting for guidance. But what would he do with guidance? This is not a maze. There is no way out. There is no riddle, no answer. There is only space. The space inside the cage and the space inside his head. The space in the cage is getting smaller and the space in his head is growing. His mind wanders to places he doesn't recognize. Uncharted territory. A girl sits in a cubicle typing on her computer. A mother stands on her front porch smoking while the kids scream and cry inside. A dog pants in a station wagon, windows cracked, radio blaring, tuned to the game. An old woman slaps an old man in a deserted park. He stays, kneeling, for hours. He thinks, please help me. Show me. Who is he talking to? To the guard, he is just another enemy, seeking the enemy god. But he isn't the enemy. He can't read the book they've given him anymore. If he had known, he would have been prepared. The one thing that might have been useful here is to know is the guttural language of the birds. What else is useful, when you only have one book?

Every day is the same now. They wake him, they take him to the room, they question him for twenty hours, and then they take him back. One day Dee is there again.

"How are you holding up?" she asks. She's worried about him. She's the only one who knows there's nothing left to interrogate him about. He's been in cages for two long. There's no value. Except that's not how he's classified. In fact, he's classified as one of only four high-value detainees. He knows this, somehow. He doesn't know how he knows anything anymore. But that's why he's kept in isolation, every move watched. She's brought him out more to check on his mental health than anything else.

"I was a pilot," he says. There. An action taken. The old him didn't talk this way. Didn't seek approval from young women. The old him didn't beg for anything.

"I know," she says, lifting her hand from a dossier, tucking a strand of hair back behind her ear.

"We followed the troops north. Our general was a man who knew how to win. An all-costs kind of fighter. He didn't separate men from their homes and stand them naked on crates. He didn't write memos. He bombed the entire city. His strategy was to kill everybody. He wanted to nuke the big guys. It makes everyone nuts, when the wars go on and on. But the president wasn't having it."

"Have you been thinking a lot about this?"

"I was never one of them. Not for a day. I was straight and neat, like you. I've always been about personal responsibility."

"Have you been thinking about hurting yourself?" Dee says. "Do you think about trying to kill yourself? With a makeshift rope?"

"Nope," he says. She's invading my space, he thinks. Invasion of space by a female. "If you're coasting, you're going downhill."

Someone kicks on the door twice but Dee doesn't flinch. "What are we talking about here?" Dee says gently. "Is there something you want to tell me?"

That's when he knows. The small concern on her face. Don't trust people, he tells himself. The furrow creasing across her forehead. It's the beginning of getting old. The waddles are coming. You wake up and look over and she's got chins like a flex hose. He hopes she's still married. No ring this time. Who would wear a ring in this place? What does he know? Why does he know it? He does. What are we talking about, she said. He's losing his wife's face. He's never going to see his wife again. He's just one person.

"Is it ever too late? Do you believe in too late?" he asks her.

"You're losing me. I'm not following you."

"I'm losing myself," he says. This is what they want! To parade a madman past the madding crowd for a public denouncement! Or maybe they believe he will pass through madness and emerge completely tame on the other side? "No one's in charge, are they?" he asks Dee. "You've forgotten why you're here."

"I'm here to serve my country."

"Good girl," Donald says.

He doesn't see Dee again for a while. The days are passing. The guards won't talk to him. Grady is long gone. He doesn't work on the confession. He writes about his wife. There should be a book about her. It's a good story, as good as his, perhaps, although of course they're intertwined. It's a book about people, not ideas. Not systems. People. Lives. What really matters. The world of intelligence is imperfect. That's the way it is in life. If you look down from Mars it's clear that the places with free systems do better for their people, and the ones with less free systems do poorly. He said that once, but the fact is he was thinking about the systems and his wife was the one who thought about the people. That's why they are so good together. That's why he needs her. He writes about her in high school, and how she went off to college in the mountains, and about the other man she dangled there in front of him until he couldn't take it anymore. She wasn't stupid. She had her systems, too. They married young but just in time. It's hard to capture her fun. She was always fun but she was always real, too.

In the interrogation room he tells the men about her. "I used to joke with her about becoming president. I tried to, you know. President. The court. They didn't work out. But she worked out. We were, what, fourteen, fifteen? And she was a little pixie. She was secretary and I was VP. She was with someone, but it wasn't going anywhere. We dated, you know, but she didn't trust me. I'd gone with too many of her friends. You know how it is when you're young."

The men look at each other silently.

"She wouldn't just follow me around. She made me come to her. Smart! She was an art major but studied politics so we could talk about it. I would have loved to play the field a little more, you know? But I thought I'd lose her."

Why don't they shut him up? The more he talks, the clearer he thinks.

"Some of our best years were abroad. We rented a van with the kids and Mom to visit her ancestral home. I ran with the bulls. She liked being the ambassador's wife."

They listen to him for a while. Then they take him back to his cell. He hopes they think he's ready.

He writes about her cooped up in their house during the snobby years in business. She didn't like the country clubs. She had always been the one focused on reaching out. *She refused*, he writes, *to let circumstance dictate her children's lives. If their scope was limited she expanded it, and if money shaped their experiences too much she forced them to reshape their world—not by making decisions for them but rather by widening the range of choices to let the innate thrill of new directions and possibilities take hold.*

He reads that back to himself aloud. That's not even my voice anymore, he thinks.

"Shall we pray? Shall we pray, brother?"

He wakes up one night to find the kid standing outside his cell. There's no guard. The light is nightclub blue. "What do you want?" he asks the kid. The day in the library seems like longer ago than childhood, too long for one life.

The kid doesn't say anything. He's wearing the same suit. It looks like he's been wearing it a long time. His shoes are scuffed too, all the shine worn off both big toes.

"History will decide," he tells the kid. "These people are trained to lie. They're trained to say they were tortured. Their training manual says so. We learned a great deal about them. Their methods. Their skill sets. We've learned a great deal through this process which has been humane."

He is falling back to sleep when he hears the voice start in softly. "Three spies," the kid says, "are in a bar." The kid squats down on his haunches. "They're having drinks and arguing over who's the best." "I've heard it," he says. "I've heard it all." "You have no choice," the kid says, smiling. "So they decide that whoever can come back to the table with a camel first wins." He starts to swear at the kid but his mouth feels funny. He touches his lips with his fingers and they come back with blood on them.

"Our guy goes out and calls up the King and says, 'King, get me a camel, now.' Ten minutes later, the King shows up with the camel and our guy says, 'Good job, King,' and runs back into the bar. But the second agent is already sitting there with his feet up on a camel."

Someone is standing next to the kid. A woman. He's brought her here to hear this.

"'How'd you do that?' says our guy. The second guy just shrugs. So they wait for a while and then take their camels and go looking for the third guy. He's in the alley behind the bar. He's got this donkey tied up to a telephone pole, and they watch him take these two big electric cables and stick 'em on the donkey's balls. There's a big *blam* and flash and the donkey goes crazy and the third spy's starts yelling, 'You're a camel, just say it—you're a goddamn camel!'"

The woman laughs. At least he thinks she's laughing. She's making some kind of noise out there. Everyone knows that joke. What is she doing here? But the kid is still talking. A father plugs in a new humidifier. A girl walks through a market, shopping for scarves. Their skeletons exposed.

"The donkey's writhing in pain. He's got a zillion megajolts going through his nuts and this crazy dude's telling him he's a camel. But he's not a camel. He's a donkey. And nothing is going to change that." The kid's alone now. He can hear footsteps out there, but whether it's one person or two, coming or going, he can't tell. "Finally he looks over at the other two agents sitting on their steeds. 'Just do it,' says the first donkey.

'It's not so bad,' says the second donkey. So the third donkey calls out: 'I'm a camel, okay, I'm a camel!' and the agent immediately locks him in this little shack. It's quiet in there at least, and there's fresh grass for the camel to eat. The camel eats. He sleeps. Every so often a soldier shows up and rides the camel to town, ties him up outside of a whorehouse, and then rides him back to the shed after a few hours. But one day a new soldier walks into the shed. He doesn't seem to know how to ride camels, and keeps trying to get on from behind. The camel keeps turning to try to help the guy until he realizes what the sicko's doing. 'Hey,' he says, 'why don't you ride to town like everyone else?' The soldier looks a little embarrassed but in the end he won't give up. He's got his pants down and is still trying this way and that way but the camel keeps squirming around, won't let him. After a while they come across three beautiful women stranded in the middle of the desert. 'Please,' say the women, 'we'll do anything for you, *anything*, if you can fix our car.' So the soldier fixes it, it's tough but he manages, and when he's done he grins up at the women for a minute. 'The three of you,' he says, 'I want you to hold this camel still for me.' But at the last minute, the donkey calls out: 'I'm a donkey!' Everyone looks at the soldier. The girls, the soldiers, the agents, the whores from the whorehouse, the bartender, the other camels. 'Give me a break,' he says. He turns to the donkey. 'Do they call me Daniel the Church Builder? Or Daniel the Savior of Our School? Of course not, but you go and fuck one donkey...'" The kid trails off with one long hand pointing off into space and air.

"I've heard it all," he tells the kid. "From better men than you." He wants a cigarette although he can't remember the last time he smoked. Sixty years ago? The kid is staring at him. The kid is not as young as he seemed. His skin is good. The largest organ in the body. What happens when it fails?

The bartender. The sheep. The one-legged man. The kid drones on and on.

*   *   *

Dee is back, and today there's a shrink there, too. You can tell he's a shrink by the way he won't stop looking at him but not in a top-dog kind of way. He's been trained. Why would they train shrinks to stare? But they do. They don't think they do but they always do.

"How are you holding up?" says Dee.

"Peachy," he says. "Hi Doc."

"Hello."

"It must be hard to tell the difference between going crazy and holding up," he tells the doctor.

"Not so hard," says the doctor.

"So how am I holding up?"

"You're doing fine."

"Things are coming to a conclusion for you," Dee says. "It's going to be soon."

"I don't even know the price of bananas anymore. How much is a pound of bananas?"

"I don't know," Dee says. "They're cheap."

"I wasn't one to hold you personally responsible," he says. "I understand systems. But right now I'm saying that you, Dee, you personally are responsible. There comes a time. You need to look at yourself and see what you've been doing."

Dee looks hurt! The doctor touches her on the arm. If only I could get her arm, he thinks. Grab the arm, drop down, grab the thigh with your outside arm, then duck underneath. If he's not fast enough, she'll just fall on top and crush him. But if he is still fast enough, then she's on your back. Clamp down on the overhook and fire down with the trapped leg. Pop the head and secure the bastard. It's an all-or-nothing move, no two ways about it. It worked for him for a long time until he ran into someone with technique that was not just better but truly superior. Then it didn't work anymore. His enemy would wait for him to go for the leg, block it, sidestep, and then nail him with an ankle pickup on the retreat. The only thing he could do was try to wear the bastard down. Just keep coming forward and hope that time didn't run out.

"I'm sorry you feel that way," she's saying. "I've tried to help you in every way I came."

"Well you've failed. Worse than that. You're messing up my system. You stupid bitch."

"I'm sorry you feel that way." Dee smoothes her hands across her lap and then folds them in front of her. "You'll be assigned someone else soon."

They take him to a new location. He is chained and shuffled out and loaded in the back of a tiny medical van. It's an oven in there. A guard sits across from him. The journey takes forever. He asks for water.

"I can't open the door from the inside," says the guard.

"Please," he says. And then he throws up. The soldier slides a bucket over just in time.

The new structure is brand new. It has barely even been finished. The cells are like dog kennels with steel bunks. There are three other prisoners there. He can see them but they can't see each other. Green plastic barriers separate them. Lit-up watchtowers with guards perched in a square past the razor and barbed wire double-helixed. He can feel the breeze on his face. The sun is setting in gold and red behind one of the guard towers. From all around him rise the sounds of the prayer call, although he sees only the three prisoners, and none of them are praying. They are watching him. One of them is his old assistant. His old assistant stares at him but doesn't blink or nod or even flinch.

The guards pull him into a room of unfinished concrete before Donald can call out.

"He didn't do anything," he tells the guards. "He just did what he was told. Like you. You and you and you."

*   *   *

The cinderblock room is cold and full of people. It's like an unfinished safe room with the AC cranked up high. The shrink is there, along with a new interrogator, very thin, and four soldiers in street clothes. Maybe they aren't soldiers anymore. But look at them. What else could they be? The purpose and resolve.

The thin interrogator starts at the beginning again. It feels like just another interrogation until he realizes he hasn't answered any of the questions. He hasn't said a word. Then the soldiers are lifting him out of his chair and carrying him into another part of the room. They place him on a table and strap him down. They lock his head in place.

"Where is he?" the thin interrogator says.

"Go ahead," he says. His voice sounds a little wobbly, a little weaker than he'd hoped. Maybe the kid is in the room. He has to be here for this. And the third man must be too. They're going to pull plastic wrap over his face and drown him. It doesn't look like much in pictures but he's heard it feels like dying. "It's what you've been waiting for, isn't it?" he says. He sounds a little stronger. "At least you'll know. Everyone will."

The thin interrogator looks down at him for a long time. And then, instead, they simply leave him there.

10

The mountains were a fine place to study art. That's what he called it: that mountain school or play school. I knew why he cast aspersions on it. He always resented the fact that I had not followed him east, and yet if I had followed him, he likely would have lost a modicum of respect for me. I certainly would have respected myself less, and I am grateful to report that my self-respect was then and has always been more essential to me than the attitudes and views of others. Some might call it pride, but there is a difference, and he always recognized it.

Beauty was an acceptable subject of study for young women in those days, and many of us turned to art history and literature. Politics and foreign policy were not forbidden, but it was uncommon to see many girls in

The tiny pencil breaks. To sharpen it, you use your nails. They used to cut them. They don't now. A new page.

The bottom line is I never would have married anyone until he married someone other than me. I'm sure he would have liked to live the bachelor's life for a few more years. But he thought: Gee, I'm not going to wake up someday and say why didn't you act faster or sooner. So it was more of an intellectual decision, not knowing that I would have waited. So the fact that we were engaged was just a big surprise to everyone. It's not that there wasn't passion. Of course there was. But it was always a lifelong partnership.

The pencil breaks again, and he throws it down, watching it skittle. What is she thinking right now? He could already be dead, for all she knows, but she doesn't think so. She can still feel him sleeping in the lower-left-hand corner of her heart. He picks up the pencil again and slowly, patiently, carves a point from it again. There is so much to tell. A flash comes from his flying days, when he would come home as frustrated as she ever saw him. He was never a good teacher. He lacked the patience. What should she write about that? Or about the boyfriends in the mountains? How much could he stand?

The jealousy creeps up the back of his tongue as if it never went away. Perhaps it never does. He looks around him at the pages scrawled. Total control. Total responsibility. He sharpens the pencil and continues.

He does not know how long it's been since they moved him to this room. It made no sense. Then again it made no sense to spend several hundred million dollars a year to defend a frozen rock with 100,000 drunks, but would they let him shut it down? It made no sense to come back on a visit and find that his father couldn't recognize him. The one illness that might be worse on the family than on the victim. It still broke his heart. A journalist once asked him about it and he started crying. War wastes everything. You can spend billions and find out in the end, you didn't need everything, and people will criticize you that it made no sense. But if you end up needing something you don't have, god help you.

Then one day they move him out of isolation. They won't let him take his book. Motes of sunlight dance in his new cell. They will keep the pages as evidence, at least, won't they? He asks the guards again and again.

"The people have a right to know," he tells them. "Sources will confirm everything. We'll declassify what we have to."

"I don't know nothing about it," says the big islander he sees more often. "Things are crazy, man. They're shutting this bitch down."

It's good to hear people talk like people again. He can feel his mind crawling back to him on its bloodied hands and knees. "When."

"Soon, soon. Soon as they figure out where to put what's left. What's your number? This must be the wrong chart."

"I can't remember."

"How long you been here?"

"I don't know."

"I hear you on that." The big islander scratches his crotch in such a joyous way that he's reminded of the fireman's throw again. Grab the arm. He looks down at his body. The skin is mottled and pale, sores on his wrist and calf. The dead iguana smell seems to be coming from his own mouth.

"I used to be a wrestler," he tells the guard. "I used to be a variety of things."

"Wrestling's weird," the guard says. "Give me some light gloves, a ring, no rules, that's more like it. We should have stopped at swords. It's too easy to kill people. Of course there really are a shitload of people."

"Are there?"

The guard squints, trying to bring him into focus. "They gave you the business, old man, didn't they?"

"Indeed, indeed."

"That's what I'm talking about. We stop at swords, how is someone like you still dangerous? You could be retired out there on a beach or wherever you people hang. We wouldn't even need to kill people like you. We could just let you do your thing until you showed up with a sword. Then we'd kill you."

"I tried to." His mouth barely works. It's been so long since he talked.

"We're winning this war, old man. Against all odds, we're winning it."

"Good," he whispers.

They let him sleep as much as he wants to now. He sleeps all the time. The heat is comprehensive. He sweats and sleeps but does not dream.

* * *

He wakes one day to the sound of voices speaking in the bird tongue. He can hear them but he cannot see them. "Deliverance is close," one of the voices says.

"He is with those who are patient."

"There falls not a leaf but He knows it."

"Shall we pray, brother?"

"Deliverance is close."

Are they planning something? "Guard!" he calls out. But his voice is still too weak.

No one will ever appreciate what he did to change the systems. The battles he fought. The effort it took to make the military stronger while curbing its political power. No one will know how limp his body was at night as it refilled its emptiness. I would go to sleep alone but wake up sometime in the night to find him half undressed, one shoe off, clutching his glasses in his hand. I never loved him more than then, because it is so much harder when you're older, with so little to gain and so much to lose. We were getting old, no two ways about it, but we still loved each other, and he still smelled of cinnamon.

There's nothing to write with anymore.

History will decide, but in the meantime, the critics are unsatisfied, and despite what's been done to him, to us, I don't think anyone could ever suffer enough to satisfy.

More prisoners are leaving. They are short-shackled, dressed in blue, and taken away. Equipment too. Cells are being cut up into pieces with arc welders and dismantled by contract vendors, stirring up storms of dust. He wants to shout something at someone. But he doesn't know how to begin.

He tries to talk to the men in the cells around him. No one tells him not to. But they won't talk to him. "Where are they taking us?" he calls out. He has forgotten their language. "God's will be done!" he says. "Praise to all lords of the world!"

The men and machines keep working and hurrying in the din.

He wakes up one morning to total silence. Is he dead? Then he hears the *toc toc toc* of the woodpecker at work. He doesn't hear anything else. He holds his breath and closes his eyes. The woodpecker stops. And then he hears something, far away, something that he could never hear before. Thump. Silence. Thump. It's the ocean. Thump. It has been there all along. He squints through wire and bars and metal. There's no one out there. They've closed the base and left him. Only him? Maybe there's someone else. *Toc toc toc*. Thump. There's still an island out there. Windswept, post-apocalyptic. Houses abandoned, empty hospitals. Then there's the rest of the island, where the island people actually live. Maybe they're already in the ruins. A father and a mother and three boys picking through the minefield and debris. What will they do when they find him? He's an old man, far from home. Will they be kind? Will they recognize him? He won't lie. He'll tell them. They will be as kind and cruel as anyone else on any given day. It will just depend. Are they in love? Are they hungry? Have they ever lost everything or been threatened and betrayed? Are they scared, proud, compassionate, armed? What is their character? Will they hand him over to their government? What kind of decisions have they had to make in their lives?

He puts his hands around the grate of the entrance and leans on it. The door clicks and inches ajar. He pushes hard with both hands and the door swings open.

Outside, the sea sways calm and blue in front of him. The sun's at the top of the sky. He heads toward the water through scrub and skinny cacti. Glancing behind him, he catches a view of the cell block sitting small and inconsequential against the island's bulk, and then he stands for a moment to take in the other cell blocks clinging to the coast in a line. More than he remembered. What else has he forgotten? Beyond his sight lies whatever's left of the base, the barracks, the stores, the airstrip, everything. They've left it all behind. But we'll be back, he thinks. He turns to face the ocean, the water and the fence, the mines in every direction. He turns and turns as he scans for a way forward. The glare is blinding, bright as snow.

NOTES

ERIC B. MARTIN is the author of *The Virgin's Guide to Mexico* and two other novels.

STEPHEN ELLIOTT is the author of seven books, including the memoir *The Adderall Diaries* and the novel *Happy Baby*. His writing has been featured in *Esquire*, the *New York Times*, *GQ*, *Best American Non-Required Reading*, and *Best Sex Writing*. He is the founding editor of the online magazine *The Rumpus*.

While this book is fiction, imprisonment details and the main character's biography are based closely on non-fiction sources, in particular *Enemy Combatant* by Moazzam Begg and *By His Own Rules* by Bradley Graham. Invaluable research was provided by 2008 McSweeney's interns Sandra Allen, April Goodman, Eric Meyers, Arianna Reiche, and Théo Sersiron.